I0653139

ALL I CAN
TRULY DELIVER

Matt Vadnais

ALL I CAN
TRULY DELIVER

COVER STORIES

Matt Vadnais

DEL SOL PRESS

❧ Contents ❦

The Great Wall   5

The Treesitter   27

All I Can Truly Deliver   41

The Seventeenth Aureliano and Jesus
    (Who Was Thirteenth in Number)   89

The Dead   107

How Bartleby Spent the Night in the Detroit
    House of Corrections Preferring not to
    Contemplate the World, Preferring not to
    Start His Life Over Again   123

Real-Time Video of Dead People You Want
    to Have Coffee With   135

About Cover Stories   203

❧ *Acknowledgments* ❧

Obviously, perhaps pretentiously, I owe a debt to the authors whose work I have "covered" in this collection as well as to the librarians and literature department at the University of Idaho for giving me the context necessary for such work. I am grateful for the guidance and instruction of Mary Clearman Blew, Lance Olsen, Barbara Haas, Charles Baxter, Antonya Nelson, Robert Coover, Sonia Sanchez, David Shields, Dorianne Laux, Melanie Rae Thon, Robert Wrigley, Kim Barnes, Neal Bowers, Deb Marquart, and Joe Geha. Thanks to Mary Ann Hudson, Matthew Sullivan, Jessamyn Birrer-Schnackenberg, Eric Wahl, Paul Cockeram, Scott McEachern, Joshua Borgmann, Andy Segedi, and Matt Schnackenberg for their gifts of good conversation and honest criticism. Thanks to Matt Blackburn for a close, close reading of the text. Thanks to the editors of the magazines where these stories originally appeared: "How Bartleby..." in *Fence*, "The Treesitter" in *New Orleans Review*, and "Real-Time Video..." in *DIAGRAM*. Finally, thanks to Ander Monson, Mike Neff, and the staff at Del Sol Press for making the process of putting together a first book as painless as possible.

For Mary Ann Hudson,
my sign and signified.

❧ *The Great Wall* ❧

This street doesn't go straight to the theater, but I don't want to get there too soon. I dislike pre-curtain mingling with my actors, and tonight my father-in-law is with me. Since he last saw me, my public persona has evolved. A year ago, I could get away with nothing more than a leather coat and a sweater. I was expected to be strange but still sincere. Tonight, my directorial costume includes a long coat, stiff gloves I can't wear while driving, and a pair of sunglasses.

When we get there, I will speak in riddles.

My father-in-law seems to understand that in the two and a half years since Abby's death, my attendance itself has become a performance. Still, he hasn't seen me in a year, and, next to his sturdy presence — a thick neck and efficient tie — I am embarrassed.

If he knows I am taking a detour, he doesn't let on. As we pass grain elevators, a golf course, and the Winter Shows Building, he gestures with his head. He doesn't say anything, but I know what he's thinking. The first time he visited Thompson he said the town was built inside out.

"All the interesting is on the outside," he said.

He only says things once.

It's been snowing all day, harder for the last half-hour, but I can't tell if the road is slick. The flakes are small and constant, the kind of snow that sticks. The side and rear windows glaze so that, in the streetlights, the air is bright and falling.

I'd like a cigarette, but I don't want him to know I started again.

"What's the last play you've been to?" I ask.

"Your last one."

He smiles and I know that he means to add that he likes theater but doesn't have time or anyone to go with back in Missouri. He means to say that he is excited, that I shouldn't worry, that he wouldn't miss the show for anything. I'm not sure if I believe him, but, because it never gets said, I don't have to decide.

He has come to North Dakota for Thanksgiving. It is eight hundred miles from Branson, where he is an administrator for a rehab clinic; he has made the trip every Thanksgiving since Abby and I took jobs here seven years ago.

Our first winter in Thompson, he asked me to direct so that the run overlapped his visit. I was able to talk my cast into a single performance the Tuesday before school let out. I have done it the same way every year though I suspect he hasn't enjoyed the tradition as much since my work started to become more unusual.

Of course he hasn't complained.

When Abby was alive, her father was just an audience member and his silence was just silence. Even the last two Thanksgivings — he and I alone — were easier than tonight; this show is the weirdest thing I've ever done, really theoretical, and I want to him have a *chance*. But there's something else, a dry-throated urgency that didn't set in until he was in the car.

I take another wrong turn, careful to stay where the plows have been.

"How much you want to know?"

"Whatever you want to tell," he says. "How much would you have told Abby?"

"Everything. Till her ear fell off," I say. "Then some more. She'd have been borrowing ears by the time I was finished."

He is laughing now, a deep shaking. He is bigger than I am, heavier every year, and the gravity of his laughter is good. "It's an odd little show," I say. I am on the verge of my practiced remarks when it occurs to me that I don't know how much he wants to understand. "It's an adaptation of a Kafka story," I say.

"So I have to go somewhere else if I want singing."

I laugh too loudly. When I stop, he stops. He sits perfectly still, his hands folded into his broad lap. I have no idea what he is thinking, but I know that if I don't say anything he is done talking.

The silence is not terrible.

I drive the snowy streets until just a few minutes before curtain.

———

I am rereading Sheridan when Abby opens the office door, a bowl of popcorn in hand.

"Let's get this straight," she says. "This may look like servitude but it's not."

"No?"

"Obviously not. It's sabotage."

"Obviously."

"Can you avoid the greasy keyboard?"

"I hate a greasy keyboard."

"I know." She leaves the bowl within reach and pulls up a stool to watch the drama. We made a rule early on that we couldn't complain about being observed: we will be busy forever and if privacy is the only way to be productive, we will never see each other. So she sits, a few feet from me, eating my popcorn.

I am directing a February production of *School for Scandal*. Part of my work this afternoon is trying to figure out how to make my pool of men stretch, but I am more interested in an essay I am writing. I am arguing that farce is maligned not because it is less sophisticated than the postmodern crap I see at theatre festivals: the post-moderns should love farce. Even before intermission, lies become easier to believe than truth; burglars, taken for butlers, have to act the part; identity is liquid. And yet, farce is treated even worse than melodrama.

I am arguing that it is the optimism of the last five minutes that make farce gauche. When it comes time to sort out what has happened, we can. We want to believe our ordeals and complications defy resolution. By looking down our nose at farce, we can blame our unsolved dilemmas on heuristics and hegemony — we don't have to fix anything.

I am underlining support in Sheridan when I hear Abby. She is chewing with her mouth open. She closes it when I look up.

"What are you doing, Mister Farce-is-Art?"

"Why are we so afraid of sense?"

"A chili dog the size of El Paso," she says. "Whiskey trees and Hester Prynne." She is willing to continue along these lines indefinitely. I am not sure if this was the purpose of her coming to the office, but I put the script down to kiss at her.

She crushes popcorn into my beard.

We don't have sex until after dinner, but we manage to make a nice mess.

———

Our pumpkin pie is mock, just tofu and pumpkin.

I don't feel right about tricking Abby's father, but I promised not to say anything. It has been just over a year since her mother left for San Francisco. He is finally seeing a therapist and it shows — he makes eye contact again. Abby thinks it will take another year to get him to see a dietician. We have spent the week teaching him tricks and recipes. I showed him how to cut saturated fat in half while browning hamburger. We made soup with salsa and three kinds of beans. We sauté with olive oil, use yogurt instead of butter.

"I'm not used to this," he has said again and again. The first few times, I thought he meant the cooking or attention to fiber.

Watching him carve the turkey, I realize that he meant something else. Our knife is not sharp, and he looses patience, pulling the joints apart with his fingers, lifting the breast meat off in jagged chunks. The bird is small, and it doesn't take long to finish. With the knife in his hand, he looks at the carcass, several bones snapped.

He is embarrassed.

I take a few strings of meat from the tray and drip them in the gravy boat.

"Tasty," I say. "Well-sliced, Zukes."

He smiles when I call him that. Neither he nor Abby will explain the nickname's origins. I have no idea what I am calling him, but I like it too.

He puts the knife down and follows me as I take the meat to the table. Abby and I jerked the turkey. I can smell how spicy it is. I go back to the kitchen for gravy and the bowl of mashed, blue potatoes.

"Tropical," Abby reminds us. "It's festive." The year before, our first in North Dakota, she called it Norsegiving and we made dumplings instead of stuffing, lefse instead of dinner rolls. Her father smiles at the yams with pineapple, but I can tell he thinks the whole thing is weird.

"Long as I get pumpkin pie," he says.

———

I am eating with Shannon Gills. Café Wittenberg is maybe not the best place to eat in Thompson, but it is the newest, opening less then a year ago, a few days after Abby died. It is essentially the same as any small-town diner with the addition of some cabbage-based entrees.

Shannon teaches intro to acting, Shakespeare, and twentieth century American drama. "You know I wrote my thesis on Wilde," she says. "But God save the community college. Where anyone can teach anything."

"It's good to be multivalent. It keeps you sharp," I say. "And it's a fun way to picket the president." I don't blink. She waits for me to explain.

When she talks, I tap my spoon against my salad plate, once for every syllable.

Yesterday, I spent an entire faculty meeting humming a patriotic medley.

I have taken to calling the rest of the faculty by numbers. Shannon is Number Four. If she is bothered, she is a better actor than her work indicates.

I am interested in how much I can get away with. I have just finished re-reading Foucault and it seems like the Panopticon ought to be able to work backwards, a crafty subject manipulating his or her observers. My peers know I'm a mess with Abby gone. How much craziness and sadness will it take before co-workers and friends write me off completely?

I want to write a personal essay about grief under observation, but, every time I start, it becomes something else.

Sometimes, like now with Shannon Gills looking at me, I have other reasons for acting strangely. It has been long enough that people are starting to feel comfortable asking questions. They are careful, clear that I don't have to answer anything I don't want to. They ask me if she suffered, if it was sudden. I say we were both twenty-nine, and they usually drop it. They ask me how it happened, and I say it was winter.

A few weeks ago, I was playing racquetball with Marv Pitman and Larry Boyd, a stranger from the statistics department. When Boyd asked me if I was married, Marv told him Abby died eighteen months ago. Boyd, seemingly out of habit, asked if we were close. I told him she was my wife, not my aunt. He started crying.

No one asks anything if I am crazy.

Still, I have to be careful; I'm not ready to go back to therapy and I don't know what I'd do if the school got rid of me.

I stop it with the spoon and, sure enough, as soon as we have our food Shannon Gills mentions Abby. She is sincere and patient, the worst kind of inquisition, the kind that knows the answers already, the kind that thinks it unhealthy not to talk about it, the kind that is trying to do me some real good.

I try to write about Abby but end up with an essay about mimesis and the curtain call.

I decide to put the Kafka show on hold again. Instead, I will direct something familiar, Simon or Williams. I won't mess with the play itself, but I will abandon the audience at the end, leave them applauding for a cast that never returns.

I haven't actually seen the reader boards until now, entering the theater with my father-in-law. The only place I could find the ones I wanted was a private high school in Fargo that had just replaced the scoreboards in their football stadium. These old signs were sitting in storage, but the school is charging us five hundred bucks a night. We couldn't afford them any earlier than now.

Though we haven't had a full tech run, I am not afraid of mistakes: the cast and crew are afraid of me. They call me Doctor Strangelove and laugh at all of my jokes. They read Derrida and Borges in my presence. A handful of disciples wear black and hone aloof nods. And everyone I work with thinks that the smallest thing will push me over the edge. Their attention to my sanity makes directing easy.

Tonight's show will be exactly what I wanted.

As we survey the theater, one of the scoreboards says "Kafka's *Great Wall of China*." The other flashes one of Kafka's parables, a few words at a time. The signs are huge, way too big for our black-box theater. We glow-taped the aisles, but with the house lights off, the digital yellow letters illuminate the room.

The set is empty but for the signs. No discernible stage. The walls have been covered with gauze so the borders of the room are indefinite. It is simultaneously industrial and expansive.

The clocks have been replaced with ornate sundials.

My father-in-law breathes in appreciation. I watch him read. He is in his only coat and tie, the one he wore for the wedding and, by the light of the reader board, I can see how tight it has gotten.

"Zukes," I say and he smiles at me. "We can sit down. It'll repeat."

He lets me lead him into the middle of the seating area.

The sign says "the Emperor has a message for you."

As the crowd parts for us, people who know me say hello. I try to respond quietly, so my father-in-law won't hear me.

"Unity! Unity!" I say. My friends and co-workers nod or laugh.

They shake my hand and let us pass.

There is bottled water and MRE under our seats. My father-in-law seems pleased with the props. He investigates the supplies and arranges the vegetable crackers and cheese spread near our feet for easy access.

———

I don't get a chance to meet her father before the softball game starts. Abby's mother didn't come with us, even after she made us wait for her to finish a phone call. She hung up and said she couldn't stand sitting on the aluminum bleachers.

"What she can't stand," Abby says, "is anyone taking interest in my father."

She waits for me to react, but I don't think it's a good idea. This is my first weekend and I am uneasy. Anything I say runs the risk of trouble, so I pay strict attention to the game.

I am surprised by her father's glove. He is squatty for a second baseman, shorter and more solid than most catchers, but he's graceful and has soft, huge hands. Everything hit to the right side comes straight to him.

Since I got involved with the theater, it has been awkward for other men to find out that I know sports. I'm no threat if I talk about wine or the color of their sweaters. Abby swears her father isn't like that, but I have my doubts. He is a good enough player that I will need to say something. I decide to do it quickly and change the subject.

When the game is finished, and his co-workers from the re-hab clinic are done with him, Abby brings me over. There is no hug because he is sweaty and out of breath. She doesn't introduce me, but he smiles and looks genuinely happy to stand next to us.

"You were great," I say when I am too uncomfortable not to.

He doesn't respond before I am talking again. "The back of your shirt says Zukes. What's it mean?"

"It's short for Erickson," he says.

I don't believe him, not even right away, but I don't laugh. Abby and her father exchange looks, but neither of them lets me know what I am supposed to do.

———

I am in our office, with the his-and-hers computers and the guest bed that has only rarely been used by guests. There is a little freezer and blender because Abby said the best home-offices came with milkshakes.

My grief — everyone says to call it that, be honest — makes it a bad idea to work in this room, but grief won't build a new house. The school says I've had enough time and popular wisdom is to get on with things. Even my father-in-law has hinted that I should be ready by now.

I am to direct the second show of the season. I have chosen *The Foreigner*, my rabbit's-foot play, the easiest of the contemporary farces. I've come downstairs, to the office, to look at preliminary set designs and review notes from previous productions. I have come to make decisions.

I have come to *conceptualize*.

In the past, I have not bothered with such things. I have argued, in essays, that the beauty of farce is that interpretation is unnecessary, that premise and happenstance trump some authorial Great Plan, that hiding in a closet or gluing a broken vase back together becomes a vital activity, that face value is restored its meaning. A pratfall is just a pratfall.

I have called farce The Church of Banality.

But, with Abby dead, I deserve a master concept.

I have been trying, in this office every night for the last week, to interpret *The Foreigner*, to make it about faith or gender or something. I've even looked for ways to make it about Abby, the entire cast in loose, brown ponytails.

I have two notebooks.

I can't look at them.

I've never really paid attention to Abby's computer, to the shape of it, the sloping arc of the monitor. I realize how beautiful and unlikely it is, elegant where mine is boxy and purposeful. When she used it, I was usually on the bed—humming, throwing socks to goad her over to me, watching. I always considered it a pencil with bells and whistles. But, now, the machine has a log of her habits, copies of her exact words, a more precise memory of my wife than I have.

I inspect the wear of the keyboard, the usual letters worn more than their counterparts. The delete key is varnished. I think about her typing, how she could edit as fast as she wrote. I turn on the machine. I make words and erase them, the first things that come to mind.

Cat.

Envelope.

Pants.

I try to find a word with no folds of hidden meaning between her and me, a word without concept, a word I am willing to let go of.

Fox.

Sandwich.

Spill.

I return to my notes where I finally admit that farce doesn't *say* anything.

I've never really directed.

I write my first notes: *I will not be a choreographer for doors.* I write it again in big, curly, epiphanic letters like *I love Steve* on a school desk. I write it again and again.

Without an audience, it seems too easy.

So I turn on my computer. I write an email.

Hon, I say. Big news.

When I hear the message bing on Abby's computer, I switch desks and respond.

Will you still do farce?

I answer. This once. *The Foreigner.* So your father can see it.

It doesn't take long, back and forth a couple of times, for me to get what I'm after and soon I stop steering the conversation while it shifts to what movies are in town and what sounds good for dinner.

————

When the phone rings, I hope it is my father-in-law. We've never been very good with conversation, but his voice is a comfort. He isn't going to therapy either. He's become the only person I talk to the way that I did two years ago, before Abby died.

My parents are afraid of calling me. When they do, it is an impossible conversation. They pretend I have always been single. If I bring Abby up, they decide to clean the house or get groceries. I am still invited for Christmas, but it is clear that if I come home I will bring an unfathomable sadness with me.

Talking to my peers is slightly more comfortable though my experiment with the semiotics of grieving has become something else, something that I must keep up at all times. My reputation has gotten carried away, and I have done nothing to stop it, dressing in shiny black and having my office-door pictures digitally altered so that my face is made of static and shadow. Universities in Fargo and Grand Forks have both suggested that I would be a welcome addition. I'm far more popular as grief-crazed artist than I was when I was dowdy and liked physical comedy. I enjoy being an enigma, but I don't like to continue the role in my house.

When Zukes calls, he says hi, and I ask how he is doing.

It is too hot where he is, too cold where I am.

———

With help from the digital reader boards, the audience discovers that the Emperor has something to say. You are a shadow, remote and hidden — the parable goes — but the Emperor has something just for you.

I watch them, mostly Intro to Theatre kids who have to write a two-page report. They pay close attention to the parable so they can ignore the rest of the show and still have notes to work with. The adults are more contemplative. Even if the second-person narrative seems hokey, they seem to take pride in the Emperor's choice. I see several people smile as they read that the messenger crowds the Emperor's deathbed. Several others knit their brow with empathy as the Emperor dies and the messenger sets out to find them.

We read that the messenger is strong and powerful, steadfast and inventive, pushing with his right arm, now his left. He uses skateboards and taxicabs. He splits the crowd with a chopping gesture, cleaves a way through the throng that has gathered to mourn. He points to the mark of the Emperor upon his breast to clear up any trouble. The way is easier for him than it would be for any other man.

But the multitudes are vast.

If he could reach the open fields, the sign says, he would fly. You would soon hear his fists on your door. But he is still in the innermost chambers, struggling for air, fighting his way through a room and down a stair.

My father-in-law seems disturbed by the message. He stops

reading and looks around. I suspect he is feeling claustrophobic. Much of the audience does the same thing, especially as they read that more courts must be crossed and, after that, more stairs. They squirm and fidget as they become convinced that it is impossible.

You must sit at your window, the scoreboard says. You must wait for the parable.

The sign is so large that people keep reading, even as the message starts over. After the fifth time a few of the words begin to change with every repetition.

Soon, the parable becomes a different parable.

Eventually, the message is composed of slogans for running shoes.

———

With *The Foreigner* behind me, I have decisions to make about what comes next. I don't have to direct for another year but the advice to stay busy was good. I've asked for another show in the spring.

I can't find a script I like. Everything with lovers is too close to the story I want to tell without being the story I want to tell. And everything has lovers. Even scripts without lovers have characters that would rather be lovers.

I have tried to write my own show, but I am not a good playwright. Every time I try, my story seems no different than a dozen others, stories I hate for one good reason or another.

So I have set up for a long night in the office. The guest bed is covered with books and extra blankets. I've brought a television — the black and white set Abby got for the bathroom — and turned it on for noise.

I've given up on reading plays.

I am reading Kafka. I used to say he was farce played at a malicious speed. Now I'm interested in something else. More than any of the stories, I would like to stage his self-consciousness, a play as precarious and stubborn in the world as his prose.

I am looking for the right way to do that when Carl Sagan interrupts. He is talking about his glass-bottomed spaceship. Abby and I shared a weakness for *Cosmos*, so I pull the television closer. I don't care about science; it is the ferocity of his desire to get me to care about science that I enjoy.

He talks about the fourth dimension. His explanation is purely mathematical, as inviting as performance theory, but I love the way he gestures, the way he hopes I will listen better than I am capable.

And then he mentions time.

He says it is the fourth dimension.

He says it is not linear.

He says we make it linear after the fact so we don't go crazy. His proof is more math and deja-vu. He has models. He tries to get me to imagine a dimension of spirals pushing out in directions I can't even fathom.

He switches to a crude series of illustrations and I shut off the television.

The theory is flimsy.

Still.

I try to slip backwards, to fall into deja-vu and end up with Abby working at her computer. I relax and meditate, focus on my breathing, but I settle for memory and memory is fickle. I try to hear her voice, her laugh — the way it sometimes comes to me when I am not ready for it. I try to smell her, the way she smelled after sleep. I try to remember how her fingers felt, touching my neck, touching my ears.

When nothing works, I try to cry. I make noise, my face

strained, but I cry in dry heaves, like there's nothing left to bring up.

Eventually, I come to rest.

My hands are on my face.

I can feel my skin, my dry fingers.

Slowly, eventually, my breathing changes.

I am touching my lips with one finger.

I trace the shape of jaw with the other hand.

I unbutton my shirt slowly, the way she used to.

I play with my chest hair, twisting it, tugging it gently.

I hear Abby tell me to take off my socks. Not the pants, I hear her say.

Leave the pants for now.

She is so tall.

I don't know how to kiss her, she's so tall.

———

After wanting to adapt the Kafka story for more than a year, I have finally gotten started on the parable. I would like to have a chorus, maybe fifteen or twenty people. I would like them to wander among the audience with the same tale — the Emperor has a message for you — set to different tunes. I would like them to crawl over the audience, drape a shawl around a neck, breathe into faces, make it jarringly intimate, invasive.

I've begun to consider Kafka himself as a parable: an artist awoke one morning from uneasy dreams to find himself transformed into an insurance salesman.

Or the other way.

In any case, the accidental transformation is my favorite of his obsessions. It is what I want to do to the audience. I want them to purchase a ticket for a play at a community college and end up something else. If I could change them into bugs, I would.

I am working when I get an email from my father-in-law. The subject line says "Southern Thanksgiving." He tells me that he found a deep-fat fryer that will fit a turkey. He has included some recipes for side dishes.

"I've made each of these," he says. "Try them and tell me what you think."

Though the holiday is eight months away, I put my work down and go online to search for an exciting use of black-eyed peas.

———

For props, I had Pitmann make a lot of cheap replicas of things around my house — Styrofoam blocks with photocopies of my microwave and toaster taped to them. There are replicas of the office refrigerator and the television from the bathroom. Most of the cast are stagehands, but I told them not to just throw the stuff around. They are to make it artful.

Among the audience, a few actors serve as scholars. They explain the process to a few people at a time. This is the principle of piecemeal construction, they say. A team of twenty can finish a small piece and return to their lives.

The scholars are prepared to answer questions. Of course, they say, it could have been done in a straight line. But it would have been slow and daunting. There would have been unanswerable questions. This is the best way, even with the gaps. In fact, they say, there are rumors that the wall is finished now, even as you can see how much remains undone.

I am watching my father-in-law. He knows more about construction than I do, probably more than Kafka did. If we have made a mistake, he doesn't let on.

My scholars tell us that the wall is the only man-made structure visible from the moon. And it was built a piece at a time.

————

Like our first Thanksgivings alone, we eat in silence. The kitchen
is a disaster. We have made enough side dishes for a small battal-
ion. Though we were talkative while frying the turkey, as soon as
the table was set we gave way to old rhythms.

The meat is juicy and bad for us. We have opened two bottles
of wine. We still haven't talked about Tuesday, about what happened when the play ended. I am looking at him, thinking about
a way to bring it up, though I don't know what to say. When he
notices me watching, he smiles in such a way that it is easier to
open a third bottle of wine and cut the pie — pecan this year —
into large pieces.

We are eating dessert when the lighter falls out of my pocket.
I expect him to look disappointed but he doesn't.

After we have stuffed ourselves, without either of us admitting
anything, we move to the garage. Snow drifts in as we smoke
with the big door open.

————

When the wall is nearly finished, Shannon Gills complains about
the fire codes. She is stern enough to startle my father-in-law.
She asks the cast who is responsible and everyone says the same
thing.

The director said, they say.

She's doing the best work I have seen from her. I added her
role at the last minute. In the original, Kafka is able to directly
assert that the emperor is dead, that the wall has been built

according to commands that no one remembers. It is my favorite abstraction of the story, but Shannon Gills' objections are as close as I could come.

She interrogates the audience. Some people get upset or embarrassed while others — my fans — struggle to defend the wall.

She asks her questions.

Construction continues.

———

On Wednesday, we do what we do every Wednesday before Thanksgiving. I do not wear black. I wear clothes I bought with Abby, a red sweater and jeans. We go downtown, to revisit the places Abby and I took him during his first two visits. We don't say that this is what we are doing, but we do it in the same order every year.

We have breakfast at Rachel's. We cross the footbridge to the duck pond. It is frozen. He has never seen it any other way. We browse the jewelry store as the technicians use hot snips and tweezers to make settings for a batch of opals they got from Idaho. We stop at the grocers to get oil for the fryer before we return to Rachel's for coffee.

I want to talk about last night, about the wall, but I don't know how.

I want a cigarette but won't let myself think about it.

The next stop is Harmond's drug store.

It was Abby's favorite. We killed hours here. It was the place we walked to if we had been having stupid fights. I've never been sure her father likes it, but the basement is full of model planes and boats. Every year we go down there first and, every year, I come upstairs to play the brainteasers.

The store has the best selection I've ever seen; they have them set up in the middle of the store. Zukes won't play them with me. I only do the puzzles that Abby and I did together; right now, I am trying to assemble a wall. It wasn't one of our favorite games but it seems appropriate after last night's show. I have the puzzle set on impossible and it might be.

I realize my father-in-law is watching.

He makes a suggestion.

It is the first time he has suggested anything to me.

As I follow his advice, we hear something from the pharmacy.

A woman about seventy has fallen.

I'm holding bricks in my hand, unable to move.

Zukes doesn't move either, but he uses his cell phone to call for help.

The pharmacist checks for a pulse.

The pharmacist closes the woman's eyes. He holds her hand until the ambulance arrives. The medics are purposeful but resigned, as if they have been called here more than once. The ambulance leaves as quickly it came. The kids behind the counter start sorting candy.

My father-in-law isn't crying but he looks close, his cheeks heavy with red. His fingers are hooked in his belt loops so I won't notice them shaking. His breathing is labored and he can't stop watching himself in the mirror behind the kites.

————

The scoreboard is off, the play over.

We are surrounded.

The wall will need to be dismantled in order for us to leave. It is eleven feet tall, ten feet deep. The blocks are not heavy but Pitmann created a complicated network of clips and Velcro. I never learned how it works exactly because I didn't think I needed to know.

It will come apart, but it will be difficult.

This was the part I was looking forward to, the part where the audience realizes what has been built, the part where the audience is entombed by my dead wife's artifacts, the part where they have to destroy what I've constructed in order to go home.

I thought it wouldn't take long for someone to get frustrated.

It's been ten minutes and no one is leaving.

Those who know about Abby have started whispering.

The rest of the crowd is not bored, not restless.

They seem to be thinking.

I suddenly don't want them here, surrounded by Abby's things. I don't want them looking. I want them claustrophobic with my grief. I want them — as they figure out what the bricks are — to panic, to struggle against the wall, to scramble over it, to trip over each other in their desperation.

But they are attentive. They are curious.

I look to my father-in-law for help. I imagine he is feeling what I am, but, as always, he doesn't give me any cues. I can't tell if he is having as much trouble breathing as I am.

I want out, but it is clear that to leave I will have to get up first. I will have to squeeze out of our aisle. I will have to make my audience move their knees and let me past. I will have to take the wall down. I will have to touch the bricks, the toaster she bought at a flea market, the television her father gave us.

I will have to do it with my audience watching.

The Treesitter

I am on my way to find Megan Lock, a wisdom I have never met or spoken to. I have decided to fly into Portland mainly because I'm not ready to go all the way to California. The airplane is robust, no room in the luckless stows above our heads. The prison in front of me has fully reclined her seat. The man to my left has consummated my armrest.

Before my accident, I would have been embellished by the lark of space.

As it is now, I am fascinated. In the air, we — people heading home, people running away, people embanked on one quest or another, many of them as oblong as mine — are part of a nice illustration. In this briefest of momentums, we are heading the same direction, suspended over everything we know in a shared, metal paragraph.

For now, we are only about flying.

I watch children whittle. I listen to biographies interspersed and exchanged as clusters of compensation open and close.

I am giddy, a lunar landing.

Since the accident, mood has become as restless as thought. I would prattle but I am not alone. If I don't complicate, I might embarrass myself.

When the attendant comes with our meals, I rub my china until he gives me the chicken.

"I ordered vegetarian," says the guy on my armrest. He is complaining to me, not to the intended. He pricks at his sandwich and I simile at him until he gets rambunctious.

"Take the meat," he says. So I do.

I have enough money to cry first crass but didn't.

Some ingredients of my journey are that symbol.

I needed to glow somewhere.

I am talking my time.

What I want with Megan Lock is far less calculus. I thirst saw her picture in an article five earrings ago. She had been living in a tree for six monks, protecting some old growth in Watering State.

That's not right.

Sometimes I know when I've got the wrong word, like flicking a marble under a curtain and realizing you've sent a rubber ball or cockroach, but most of the time it's a long curtain and there's no way of checking.

She had been photographed, high in her spruce tree somewhere in Washington. I saw the article over lunch when I still worked for Moody, Moody & Pants. I didn't wrinkly look at her, didn't save the picture or anything like that. Acutely, all I remember is how uncomfortable she looked. It was obvious the photographers had her poisoned, one arm on a basket, her legs crossed, head crocked. In the other drawing, she had been stood on one flat, hanging on branches to dangle her body away from the tree.

There were no good shows of her eyes.

I barely skinned her story because mine was mostly in order. I had my mortgage paid off before forty-five and was starting to believe I understood why I had turned down graduate stool and experimental mathematics for a statistics jog in Boston.

When I said something, I said something.

But there was the accident, and by the time I saw her picture again, I was sick enough of myself to truly real about someone else.

The accident was something no one could complain: a freak explosion at work and a piece of ceiling burrowed in my sulk, into my brain. I was lucky and unlucky, the experts sped. I was able to move normally, as coordinated as effort. And I received a handsome sentiment. I would be wealthy forever. But words had become their own animals, no more partial to me than the weather.

I was waiting for an appointment at the linguistic pathology lab at M.I.P. when I saw Megan Lock again. She was no more perfect than before, hard and disquieted, a square haircut and jawbone. She had won in Washington and moved on to a new gambit in California, a strand of redwood. It was rumored, the article said, that her legs had grown sour, that it was a struggle for her to endeavor on land after so many years spent in pedestals. The article included a brief bio but lectured more about Green, Green Planet than it did about her.

She, the story said, didn't believe in doing interviews.

I began to slop, utterly sob, in the wanting room.

For the next few days, I couldn't break weeping, couldn't shake my jealousy in her something that needed no explication. I still considered her politics silly. But I bought the trinket to Portland.

———

When we are on the ground, the airplane becomes less comforting. I am not as impatient as everyone else. Time is odd — more like memory or swimming — when you know you won't need to talk about it. I watch people remember their schedules and antelope. They pack and hold their beige to line up for the exit. It is no secret that airports are unwieldy palaces but, really praying attention to what people say to each other, the place is truly frightening.

I am staying in a nearby hotel. I have a reservation but it takes a few tires to get my name right. In my room, I spend drowsy movements thumbing through the Old Testament because it has been a wrong time since I've been near one. Reading is easier than sparkling but I am slow and the effort slips neatly into dreams that are lesson like dramas than flow charts or equations, names begetting names, words begetting words.

In the morning I take a cab to a dealership and buy the first car I trust to drivel the coast. I have never sheen the Pacific so I follow the ocean south. In more ordinary times, this would be a nice vacation — less rain than there should be, foam thick enough to spread with a night, a devil's punchbowl and a whale sounding south of Lincoln City. It is not an unenjoyable drive but, without tinkering about how I would describe the sunfire, the scenery flattens and my days bend and swell like records played at the wrong speed.

For a while, in Boston, I had someone to talk through. I bought a dog and beheld him Dog. He was a border collie-sweatshirt cross and had no idea I was hard to understand. When I told him to sit, or spit, or shellac, or whatever I told him, he did what I wanted as often as any dog would. We watched baseball and I spoke to him. I told Dog long and confiscated starfish, how I had been held up in terrific, what I was like as a kid glowering up, what I was hopping for in a sanctuary.

Eventfully, I took Dog for a walk, the same rout as always. There was, as there almost was, a fenced-in dog that had been de-barked, nothing left but a cusp of wind. Dog, as he always did, didn't pay any attention to the muted grinnings or warnings or whatever they were, but it occurred to me, for the first time, that God considered the voiceless dock dead.

The next day, I put up signs. I didn't slave over the wording because I included a peep show of the dog in black and white.

Whatever I said, I got several warbles.

I think Dog is called Buddy now.

It is raining, a gray pessimist, when I finally make it to the Green, Green Planet encrampment. There are three volunteers, two men and a woman, guarding Megan's Redwood. Even for the car, my hands are cold. If they know I hem here, they do not seem to beguile. They make food over a series of gas stoves and use an elephant, a hand-operated pulley system, to whistle a full plate into the tree. The tree is sequined, dense enough to hide a Buick, so I can't see Megan Lock. Her team sends up dry clothes and an umbrella before sitting around a picnic table.

I am trying to figure out how to yodel to them when they begin taking terms with cigarette and a lighter. The woman inhales and sees me. She holds her smoke and raises a barn in my dialect. She does not blink or say anything to her fiends. She does not exhale, as if she is daring me to breathe first.

I decide to get some sleep before talking to them.

I find a hotel twenty minuets from Megan's tee and, almost immediately, become ashamed that I was intimidated. Many of the math guys I knew back in school dropped acrid to become numbers, to avoid numbers, or to pry at numbers without all of the rules. I never did. It was the rules I was interested in: multiplication, decision, all of them. I found numbers, by myselves, petty dull.

I am still not sure what it is that I am after out here but, as the rain stops beside of my hotel rune, I settle on the immediate goal of drug use.

I begin to wonder if it takes a brain trauma to really change.

All my trifle I had lived as a Yankees flag but, sometime after the accident, I finally became determined to root for the Red Songs. I convinced my former firm to grin me season tickles to

Fenway. When I realized I didn't have the courage to charm any-more, unsure of what I was screaming, I gave the seats to a home-less shelter.

I flip tunnels on the television, looking for a late-night delete about nature versus nature. Nothing like that is dancing, so I try the Old Testament again. With a mystic marker, I underline ev-ery squire I can find about ontology.

If that's the right word.

For a year after I didn't die I had therapy to remind me who I was. My sycamore canceled our sessions when I started shaving and brushing my teeth again.

Science was less interested in letting me go.

My trouble, the doctors said, was with Broker's area. That's not right. Broca's area. There was, they said, nothing they could do to help. Antidepressants, medication for headaches, but noth-ing about the worms. They shed we don't own anything about the brain really, can't figure much out without experiments. And we can't have experiments without volunteers. They couldn't even predict how bad my aphasia would bra, how often it would fare up, when it would proceed.

So I lent them study me.

People who knew what was rotten couldn't get enough of me. I put Legos together for them, answered their questions, identified thumbnails and doorknobs. I did interviews with graduate stu-dents and novelists. When I spoke, there were tears and the right kind of nodding, but I couldn't shake the future that it wasn't what I sad but how I didn't say it.

———

I leave for the encampment early the next morning. Before shift-ing town, I buy a small wardrobe of flavors other then denim. On the dive to the tree, I plan a series of opening jokes, try to invent a Green past to impress them.

When I arrive, one of the men is gone. There is still no sine of Megan Luck except for the extra set of dishes and surprise. The centuries are smoking grass again. I decide not to waste any more climate.

I will try silence.

As I approach and sit with them, I realize how out of price I am. It is not just age. They are in their late snowshoes, I think, but it is hard to tell because, however bold they are, their fiascoes have been angry ones. They look windswept. They possess a leanness that, as I am being studied, makes me feel soft. The man has a full bramble and the woman is sturdy, as chilly as it is, without sleeves. Her arms are gilded and well-muscled.

The woman offices me the joint.

I am clumsy as I take it, an embarrassment I have in the past saved only for sex. No matter how awkward I am, no one fires anything so that, as we pass the trophy, I am allowed to remain Cyprus as long as I can.

I see they had oatmeal with fruit, probably raincoats, for breakfast.

They have a fire that creaks begrudgingly.

Every time I have seen a redwood in a picture it has been sunny. Because our sky is obstinate, there is no sunlight to give texture to the bark. Megan's tree looks smooth and clay. They have tied a basketball ship to its truck.

"Hello," the woman says when I have looked long enough.

"Christopher Otto," I say. I suspect I say Christmas Otter or something equally erudite.

"Eliphaz," she says. "This is Bildad. You saw Zophar yesterday."

"Not your real flames," I say.

"Legally no," she says.

"What's legally?" asks Bildad. He is a little man with a toss of momentum, even as he sits.

"Metaphor," says Eliphaz. "Job's buddies from the Bible. Took care of him in the valley and all of that."

"I know the story."

"Every one knows every story," Bildad says.

"Right," I say. "But that one. You're acting for trouble."

"Nah," he says.

"Boils and heartache," I say. "It's a bad lethargy."

"Scars are never bad," says Bildad.

"Job wins in the end," Eliphaz says. "And we all share the Earth as it should have been."

When I don't perspire, Bildad pretends to hum.

"How is Joe?" I ask.

"How are any of us?"

"Job's good," Eliphaz says. She has very little air, cut above her ears. Her teeth watch too small in her mouth. Even as she smokes, she explores me. "She's good."

Bildad continues to hum, scraping at the tram with his fingernail.

Eliphaz exterminates the antacid.

Bildad begins to roll another.

I story the tree. Without texture and death, it flirts like something hollow and portable like a mobile home or silo. I wonder if Megan Lock can see us, if she brothers to lurch when someone new arrives, if she pays attention to Bildad as he strumpets with the morning fire, if she cheers when the others play horse.

With her closer to heathen in a tree that could dress as a tower, I think that Babel would have been a better allegory. But, I support, that story wouldn't have shuddered them with bit roles.

"How sky is she?" I ask.

"She's up there," Eliphaz says.

"Takes about a minute," Bildad says, "to get the lift high enough. Two if it's windy."

We flow silent again.

Coming here, I had imagined them chatty with a guitar and fork songs.

"Can you hear her?"

"If she screams," Eliphaz says.

I try to think of more conversion but their terse is wearing on me. I worry about driving after the pot. When I went to bars in Boston, I used my speech as a barometer of sobriety. Now I can't tell if I flee any differently than before.

Bildad starts to ridicule the table with his balms.

Eliphaz is chewing at her thumb, still dragging at me.

Neither of them saddle when I get up to leave.

Driving, I think about the Rusty Nail, a simple neighborhood ditty where the beer was cold and the sandwiches were exactly how you'd expect them. On afternoons I didn't work I would mold there and say the same things I always said in older to get the same laughs.

After the accident, I tried to sacrament but the script kept changing.

———

Back at the hostile, I re-read Job.

I think they've got it wrong.

Histrionically, Zophar and the others were a hindrance. To make it a gentle metaphor they should be talking Job down. Or convincing him to jump. And Megan is choosing her suffering, nothing to do with God at all.

It occurs to me that I would make a better Joke than Megan Lock is.

Still, I don't blame them.

A shared agenda makes bad readers out of all of us.

After blizzards, in Boston, I worked the streets with a shovel lacking for stuck or plowed-in steamboats. While I helped out I could complain about the wind-chill or flowerbox. On the coldest days, even if I left the words wild, strangers would commiserate.

Using a different colored pen than the night before, I scour and circle stories about community. There is nothing about building roads or rehabilitating the mail. There are only golden statues and wayward flogs. It occurs to me that, in the Babble, every time people start talking to each other they do something sinful or senile.

Heavy-harped, I wobble the rest of the day and, before I am ready, find myself in dreams where instead of speaking, people spit currency from countries I've never been to, coins shaped like the ones that, as a child, I begged my father to save for me.

In the morning, I leave the hotel earlier than the day before.

I stop to bribe a bag of organic marshmallows.

When I think about her now, Megan Lock has no inspiration that she is anybody's Job. It is typical that she no longer believes in the movement. She might not even remember why she is in the tree. I imagine her up there, happy with her quiet perch, reading or listening to a radio that won't fall all the way in. I imagine that even when the sky is forecast the light has a sober quantity to it, something gold and worth starring at. Or maybe she does nothing but remember. I imagine she must do a lot of dwelling, recalling people she should have kinked, recovering what she should have said.

When I get to the tree, Zophar and Eliphaz are playing chess.

He is taller than the others, clean-shaven in a Cleveland Browns stocking cap. He doesn't seem surprised at my arrival.

Eliphaz smiles at the oranges.

"I knew we had an Elihu," Bildad says.

"I'd scamper for Otto," I say.

"Come on," he says, "trust your Bildaddy. Always figured Elihu for kind of pudgy."

"No offense," I say.

"None taken."

They are no tardier than the day before but the long droughts of silence feel less staccato. We sit for a long fitness. Now and theater, Zophar tells pokes from a routine I reconcile as early Eddy Murphy. Bildad gossips about the suburbs and the cosmos. Chess games end and begin again.

Evidently, they start to make lunch. Eliphaz doesn't present me from chopping carrots or using the elevator to send Megan her fool.

"Why doesn't she chew interviews?" I ask.

"She doesn't talk much," Zophar says. He is adjusting the rain traps above the tents.

"What is talk?" Bildad yawns.

Eliphaz stops working and freckles at me. She is in a flashier shirt than yesterday but doesn't pretend any gentler.

"Megan hasn't said a thing. Not in a long time," she says.

I am not sure if she's being homage but she scenes sincere.

"Not even on shore leave," she says. "In-between trees."

After she fishes, the others continue shopping and checking. I am sobbing amends.

"What's his thing?" asks Zophar.

"Man," says Bildad. "Lay off. The guy can't talk right. Shell-shocked vet or something."

"Man," says Zophar.

Eliphaz looks at me. She isn't fragile, or even kind, but I know she understands more than the authors.

I wash dishes.

We half-heavily play basketball though it becomes evidence that only Zophar can score.

When I start for my car no one is surpassed.

In the hotel I hide the Bible for silence. I have green ink but nothing gets underlined. I have to shuttle for making note in the margins when Yahweh held His definite tongue.

I no longer envy Megan Lock's science. There are a dozen ribbons I can think of for her not talking but I no longer take it as faith. Perhaps this is why I can no longer puncture her in the tree. I can not she the shape of her shoulders or guess the length of her hair.

I have better luck when I spectate about her past. I start with the certainties. I can count on the time she learned her bicycle, left a rent in somebody's car, tore a tooth, stubbed the toes that everybody stubs. The specifics are easy to procure. I decide she is from Iowa and went to prom with a stubborn fencer who couldn't trance. I invent a father who spoke by fixing her motorcycle, a brother who never beat her at wrestling.

———

Every day, I bring something nice for the champ and we sit in the rain. I hemp out around the stove. When I am there I am the only fun to give anything to Megan. I send her carefully estranged plates, clean crowbars, bankers to keep her wan.

Zophar beats us at basketball and Eliphaz deserts him in chess.

I stay longer every time but no one experts that I would stem the night. I exaggerate that I could do their laundry and the three of them let me. Even if no trickname sticks to me and I am never one for them, they are glad to see me in the morning.

At night I search the Book for family and monkeys, faith and epistemology. I use different pens. I weave circles, underlines, wavelengths. I am not an elegant concordance but I leave detailed knots.

And I invest Megan Lock. I conduct a mother and first marriage that didn't take. I provide a fishing trip and a serious of lost kites. When Eliphaz or one of the others tells me something I was wrong about, that she was really from Utah, I am more than willing to adjust my daguerreotype.

I am not sure love is the right word.

One morning I buy a bicycle, the same contour as the one I think she leaned on in Utah. It is collapsible, blue enough to fit on the barge. I work on a note to explain myself, writing and re-wiring it but nothing says what I won't. I decide to trust she will remember how the buck kicked when it shouldn't have, how she skimmed her knee and tore up the neighbors' rhubarb. If none of these figs happened, I hope she has something better.

When no one is witnessing, I lift the bike into the tree.

I highlight trust and security, art and incoherence, memory and exfoliation.

Eliphaz takes Zophar's truck to visit her sitter. She resumes a few days later with peasants for all of us. By then I have given Megan a fishing pole and a cheeseburger with extra mustache, just the way she might like it.

Zophar teaches me a jump shot and Bildad shaves. He is hard to reconfigure without the bear. He adheres taller, his cheeks with a different angel to them, his skin a more regal pallor. Even his voice teams to bellow a half-stump higher.

I give Megan a phone book and a walking stick craved from minestrone.

Zophar sets up a volleyball fence so he can bleat us at that.

After sending a microphone, playing cards, a dolphin and herb garden, a kite, a night light, a recorder and thong book, an atlas — some rope so she can hang stuff in the biscuits if she is running out of room — a player-piano and leprechaun, a seven-inch single of what might be her favorite band and the best tasting rack of lamb I have ever sat, it seems inevitable that I give her the Bible. I include a note that says "I'm not a monastery."

Bildad tries calling me Big Fuzzy but no one likes it.

When Megan sends down her laundry, it is clutching the Bible. She has made her own notes but I can't swim the writing. I give her more rope and start to mend her twice a day.

When I arrive on a Thursday, some time after tailor day, men from the luggage company are already smoldering. I have brought lox and toasted tissue paper, but Eliphaz tells me the play is over.

"Megan?" I ask.

"She just needs to sign the paper."

The others let me send up the contact.

"No shortage of forests," Bildad says.

"I need a month," Zophar says.

Eliphaz spends the day rafting with her mouth open, her voice brighter than I have heard it.

I bribe time by laughing with the others, but when they aren't looking I send up gifts of grass and sandals, everything I can fly.

I don't tell them anything.

Megan Lock will descend to a hatch of writers and a stenography crew.

She will barely be table to walk as she declines curfews.

She will see me and we will enhance as we smuggle our first words to each other. Or she will have flip to say and more trees to forage. Or she will task me to come with and work the intercom again. Or we will magpie off to an ocean she might have seen as a child.

In the sand, if she wants, we could build skyscrapers and crêpes.

❧ *All I Can Truly Deliver* ❧

If it live in your memory, start with this line.
—Hamlet's advice to the players

Not until now, two hours after we lost an engine and our instruments, have Mary and I had a room to ourselves. Even for a submarine, the sleeping quarters are tiny. Three steel-framed bunks are lined up head-to-foot with mattresses that smell like old fruit. She sits behind me, her legs around my waist, her forehead on the nape of my neck.

As scared as the others are, they still laughed when the old man suggested Mary and I find a place to talk.

"Say it slow," said Tak. It was the first we had heard of his real voice in some time. His earlier words had been burdened with the weight of prognosis, how much air, what was broken, how much longer. But he made the joke, even managed to crack himself up, snot catching in his throat. "I may have some words for one of you later," he said. "Any of you."

Mary and I, fully clothed, haven't spoken. I am listening to her watch click in the bulkhead's pinched echo. I can't hear her breathing, can't feel it through the fabric of my shirt, but the weight of her head is real enough.

During a grassy summer before we were married, we made the

same promise every couple makes. No one gets left alone. I was never sure if we meant it but we struck the deal and she rubbed my cheeks yellow with flowers. We left our underwear hanging from an oak tree. If we were lucky enough to die together, ours would be a frantic, kissing death. So much crying our hair was wet.

No one has cried down here.

This far from sunshine and newsstands, it is impossible to play by normal emotional rules. Sometime after Tak said we were in trouble, I stubbed a toe, maybe even broke it, but I didn't cuss. The ache is a throb now, spreading up my leg but I think it would hurt more in London.

I've got fear, but even that is vague, like bags under my eyes, a symptom more than a feeling. If the others are more lucid they are no more vocal. Even Mary is quiet and she's never been a mess over anything. She is barely able to keep her head a steady pressure against my neck.

Air goes bad just as fast in silence.

I am guessing.

I am not a scientist. I only came along to film the last expedition of our famous old man. Because both of his names are hard to pronounce — two Vs in one, three Gs in the other — no one bothers to say them. He speaks in an accent. Mary said he is Swiss, though it seems that science has become its own nationality. Luckily, he answers to anything. Omar calls him Professor. Tak gets away with Pops.

When we first met, days ago at a Mexican restaurant in Nova Scotia, his handshake was easy and anonymous.

Withdrawn.

"I'm the old man," he said. I believed him. I could hear his tongue stick in his mouth as he talked. His chin was abnormally sharp, his head unfortunately egg-shaped. All of his hair was gone, save too-dark eyebrows. He seemed out of place, lingering too long, as if his body were a raincoat he had been wearing several months after a storm.

When conversation came around to the sea, he was new again. His eyes changed shape and he spoke recklessly, more gambler than scientist. Mary told me he only gets that way for the ocean or a book. And the Beatles, she said. She said he sometimes jokes about the similarities between his work and theirs. All the screaming girls.

I am the only member of the crew who has not worked with him before. As we ate our burritos, it only took a few hours to forget I hadn't. When he spoke of his life — sperm whales off the coast of Antarctica or an oil spill in the South Pacific — he let me believe I had been with them; he was simply remembering it for both of us.

That's what he does, Mary said. Give him a chemist, a hydraulics engineer, and a guy who likes to drink wine and he turns them into a research team.

In her metaphor, I was the wine guy though I'm not the only one of us who studied something other than science in college. Mary picked up a minor in dance. Tak has a degree in lit. Even the old man plays several instruments and writes poetry in the margins of his expedition logs. But it's not the same with the rest of them. Hobbies.

My only job, with my cameras and sound equipment, was to record. Before the trouble started, the task was important enough. Only Omar was difficult. Mary warned me. He's rough with beginnings, she said. A sweet guy, but pragmatic, the kind who won't piss until he's got a better reason to get up. He scowled as I loaded the trunks of lighting equipment into the sub. Mary said she didn't know if he even talked to his wife. Maybe to check the temperature of the oven, she said, but nothing without data.

The others were glad to have me. Tak told me to make him look crafty. The old man said to film whatever I wanted. I was getting good footage, the old man chewing his nails, Mary being amazing over charts and graphs.

Now I have nothing to offer anyone.

These minutes are the hardest when reduced to basics: what we have done, or not done, how much I still don't know about her, the stupidity of a single, leaky hose. Statistics about oxygen. How Mary lied to a friend of hers so I could get the BBC job. How she later got me a gig filming her crew. How she turned down a fellowship in San Diego for this. All of the Saturday crap we would be watching on television if we were Somewhere Else.

More than anything, I want her to talk. I want her to describe a dog she saw in the supermarket or tell stories about her sister's children. I try to work out a sentence only to realize that I am once again going over the facts.

Before our departure, there were rumors that the old man was terminal, a couple of polyps the size of acorns removed from his stomach, cancer in his endocrine system, the same that killed his wife. When we boarded, Mary helped him fit several personal oxygen tanks into a storage locker. Tak told stories about the hospital. Even Omar offered things we didn't know.

But, for the first ninety minutes of odd lurches and emergency power, no one said anything that wasn't related to the sub. Before Mary and I were given permission to leave, the last half-hour was all small talk—like the five of us were strangers in a deli.

I decide to move. I squeeze Mary's foot. The massage starts as tender pressure, but after working her calves, it changes. I tickle at her ankles and wiggle her kneecaps with my thumbs. Without lifting her head, she begins to tickle back. "Monkey's got the giggles," she says. She starts with the fat on my sides and moves to my armpits. We aren't laughing but it feels better.

We're still at it when Tak speaks from the other side of the bulkhead. "Tell me I'm interrupting something," he says.

"Close your eyes," Mary says, "and come in."

"I'm gonna cheat."

"And we're going to disappoint," she says. "Something?"

"Maybe." He shrugs, licks his teeth. "The old man says we're gonna do *Hamlet*."

"As in *Hamlet?*"

"No. The other one."

"Great," Mary says. "Death and acting on the same day."

"Except for Champ," Tak says. "Pops wants to film it."

"Seems silly," I say. But I am already excited. It will be easier to dwell on loving Mary without facing her.

"Do we have a script?"

"No," Tak says. He cleans his glasses, rubbing the lenses. His shirt, covered in grease, can't be helping. The shirt says *I Know More About Submarines Than You Do*. "Pops says we don't need a script. We'll know it when we need to. Something like that."

"Make it up."

"Tomato. Big, red round thing."

When we stand, Mary puts her arm around me, our hips pressed together, her right foot on my left.

"You take one leg, I'll get the other," she says.

Tak does a fatigued little mambo as he leads us to the control room. He is Korean. He wears homemade T-shirts. His hair is longer than a musician's. Though he doesn't mention it, his degrees are ivy league. Mary said he could have had a spot on any research crew. She also said, based on a letter she saw, that she thinks he's an ordained minister. If he is, he keeps it quiet. I've been meaning to bring it up, but he was busy and now doesn't seem right.

He sings us down the corridor. Marvin Gaye. His voice is thin but in tune.

We enter. The old man is using one of my spotlights to make a shadow play against reinforced glass. Behind his birds and rabbits is the blank canvas of the ocean.

"Champ came here to make a movie."

He doesn't mention death or meaning or our last few hours. The silence is a dare. At first, no one takes it. Omar cracks his thumbs by squeezing them inside his fists. Tak clicks a nail against his teeth while he hums.

Mary is less kinetic. She drapes my arm over her like a shawl. I remember yard work the morning before we flew to Nova Scotia. I pulled weeds, and she was ready to cut the grass so Ginny with the paper route would only have to do it twice while we were gone. The mower wouldn't start. Mary pumped the manual fuel injector, checked the gas and oil, and changed the spark plug. She got me to lie down and fiddle the choke with my thumb. After several minutes, the mower still didn't work. Nothing could be done, but we continued to worry about it for another hour. We made phone calls and searched the Internet. I found a crazy person that claimed our problems could be solved by mixing decaffeinated coffee with the gasoline. Mary thought about it, holding her mouth like she's holding it now. She asked me to brew a full pot so we could have some with sugar while we finished breaking the machine.

I am in love with her willingness to follow suspicious advice.

We wait and look at each other while our instruments make useless noises and Tak clicks his teeth and the old man breathes audibly until Omar is no longer able to keep his mouth shut.

"We should be fixing shit."

"No dice." Tak says.

"Then we should do what we came to do."

"Impossible," Tak says.

"If we're already dead," I offer, "we might as well do this."

"If," says Omar.

"We could do porn," Tak says.

"Look," Omar says. "We still have if."

"Not our if," Mary says.

She waits for someone to argue with her. She waits too long. I can see her grow uneasy with her own implications.

"My vote," Tak says, "we hang onto the if and shoot the movie."

He talks too fast, every bit as desperate as the way Omar bends and jerks his fingers long after the knuckles have finished popping.

"Look at it this way," Tak says, "we survive and we keep the tape, show our family like a pie-eating contest from summer camp. Or maybe we use it as an audition tape and next year the five of us stroll down the red carpet at the Oscars. But I don't dig on Hamlet. Pouty bastard. Luke Skywalker without droids. We should do *Canterbury Tales*," he says. "Or Shaft."

Mary laughs and Tak stops.

"This is not why we're here," Omar says.

"We can," I say. I have the floor. I am the man who works with film. I should have words about legacy and purpose and immortality. "This can make sense," I say.

I can't tell if anyone believes me.

"This," Omar says, "if nothing else. Listen to me. If nothing else."

He is taller than the rest of us.

"It, if nothing else, is bad science," he says. "And a bad idea."

Mary, Tak, and I try to find a better argument. After a claustrophobic minute, we turn to the old man.

"A strange thing happened to everyone I studied with," he says. "When they knew enough, they all went mad as artists. Gets to a point, you talk like a painter. Most experiments, they look like sonnets, a turn after the second quatrain."

He pauses and I study him. I wish the cameras were rolling. He doesn't have the energy I saw in Nova Scotia. His skin is sallow and he breathes with too much effort, like his whole body is yawning. But he is more impressive than I have seen him, with more gravity than I imagine him having, even as the younger man in his and Mary's stories.

"There is little difference," he says, "between us and a group of actors. Vocabulary. Mere syntax."

He swallows.

"Schumpert, the great man. No one studies him now. A great man. A sense for whales. Kinship. Could read them like the hairs on his arms. Do what you will, he told me, but leave notes like you're listening to Jesus."

No one speaks to his riddle.

"But *Hamlet?*" Tak says. "Really white, that Shakespeare."

"We could write something else," I say.

"Something new," Mary says.

"Everyone does *Hamlet,*" Tak says.

"Are these oceans new oceans?" the old man asks.

"Not why we're here," Omar says.

"Bad science," the old man says, "is leaving more mysteries than we started with."

"*Hamlet?*" Tak says.

"Ours is a tragedy."

He is so gentle when he says it.

Scene I. — Elsinore. Outside the castle. Winter.

(We cover our instruments with a sheet. I send the others to gather everything white — long underwear, handkerchiefs, tennis shoes, the apron Tak wears when he makes our meals. We bury one of my gobos to make a glowing pile of laundry.

I try to set up quickly but I am going to get this right. The others work out lines from the old man's suggestions. He outlines scenes and gives them motivation.)

BERNARDO/MARY—

Who's there?

(It doesn't seem fitting that the jewel of Western Drama should begin like a knock-knock joke. But the old man swears.)

FRANCISCO/TAK—

Still me baby.

(He looks directly at the camera.)

Ray-Ray and Big Steve. No worries. Post-colonial.

(He turns to Mary.)

You're on time. And praise Jesu. 'Tis colder than your mamma and my heart is blue.

BERNARDO/MARY—

The clock has struck twelve. Get thee to bed, Francisco.

FRANCISCO/TAK—

If you'll come.

BERNARDO/MARY—

'Tis not the time.

(She is so coy that I find myself wondering if she could sleep with him. I have never seen my wife act.)

Have you had a quiet guard?

FRANCISCO/TAK—

Even the fish are chill.

HORATIO/OMAR—

(He enters from behind me with the head from one of our dust mops for a wig. I have no idea how Tak got him to wear it.

He holds notes from the old man like a blind man's cane. Even in his ridiculous getup — Horatio has blue hair — Omar is a serious-looking man.

He too, begins by making eye contact with whoever will see this.

His words are slow, long pauses between every utterance.)

My wife is sleeping.
My kids aren't awake.
And you want me to see a ghost.

(He begins to read the old man's words. His voice is flat but not boring.)

I pray you sirs what say you? Are there any tenants in our graves this eve? Doth the wind teem with the lofty and shrill-sounding throat of the sheeted dead?

(He manages to convince me, in spite of himself. If he's acting, he's good.)

FRANCISCO/TAK—

Man. Don't mess. You set him straight Bernardo-man.

BERNARDO/MARY—

I will, with your permit, once again assail your ears that are so fortified against our story of what we two nights have seen.

(She never lets me film her about the house. She claims she ends up gray. I've never thought so, but I've never argued. She is the only subject I have no interest taping. When I see her, I want to hear her stomach gurgle, to smell her morning breath.

I am glad to be filming her now. Just in case. Though I would gladly trade everything I will get here for a ten second movie of her fishing a spoon out of the garbage disposal.)

For two nights, we have seen a figure t'would pass as the very
fashion of our now dead king. His visage did bring me pause.
Francisco can confirm the likeness.

FRANCISCO/TAK—

Not saying like. Mofo *was*. King Hamlet.
I know, I know. You thinkin' how can I tell.
The eyes, baby. Dude wore his beaver up.

HORATIO/OMAR—

Proof?

FRANCISCO/TAK—

Check this.

*(He hits a button and turns on the spot lights I installed outside the
sub. I am surprised they still work. The ocean glows.*

Before the trouble, it was no more mythical than an aquarium.)

What can't be out there?

You say you see Jesus, I'll hedge my bets and cross myself.
You say Jackie O swam by, I'll ask you what she was wearing,
was her hair cute.
What can't be out there?

BERNARDO/MARY—

(She is looking at me. The lines her and the old man had planned don't make sense. She shrugs.)

Last night, when this same tide did swallow up our course to illume this part of heaven, Francisco and myself did see from this same portal, —

FRANCISCO/TAK—

Hold up.

(He gestures to the ocean. I am only getting the back of his head. The old man is waiting, dusted in flour for his entrance. I am tempted to stop the scene. Not even Hamlet's ghost can be filmed both in and out of the sub. But the old man sits down.)

It comes again. 'Tis monstrous unnatural. 'Tis whack.

BERNARDO/MARY—

In the same figure. Mark it Horatio.

HORATIO/OMAR—

(He crowds at the glass. I have to slide the boom mic closer.)

It could be anything.

FRANCISCO/TAK—

You art a scholar, right? Speak to it.

BERNARDO/MARY—

It would not be spoke to. The devil doth have visage but not voice.

FRANCISCO/TAK—

None of that. Question it, Horatio.

HORATIO/OMAR—

(The old man stops us. He offers new suggestions.

Am I doing alright, Mary asks. Brilliant, I say. I try to use her accent but it is awful on me. She laughs and I keep it. Smashing, I say. I always fancied Bernardo as something of a git. But now, I say, he's dreadfully striking.

Even Omar laughs. I watch him crowd over the script and change a word. More acidic, he says.)

What art thou, that usurp'st this time of night? What art thou that would test my patience? Speak. Confirm the madness of mine eyes.

(Murder, the old man whispers to me. Murder most foul, blub, blub.)

You must speak. Dead or not, you must tread something more sturdy than water. How many fingers am I holding?

FRANCISCO/TAK—

Lo, you piss it off. See how it flies from hence.

(I almost believe that something is out there.

He turns to the camera.)

I mean, damn, it swims like a mother.

BERNARDO/MARY—

How now, Horatio? You tremble and look pale: Is not this something more than fantasy?

HORATIO/OMAR—

Before my God,

(He stops his line. His earlier heaviness returns.)

It was nothing monstrous.
I can tell you everything that swims out there. English or Latin, your choice.

BERNARDO/MARY—

Fuck your science, Horatio. Death cares not.

HORATIO/OMAR—

But with mine eyes I have seen, and in seeing verified. 'Tis monstrous nothing.

BERNARDO/MARY—

(She looks to me as if to apologize. She thinks for a moment and regains her composure.)

An ocean deprived of its monsters would be sleep without dreams.

(This was from the old man. I am pretty sure this is really Steinbeck but, after Tak's smooth-talking, Korean sugar-daddy Francisco, who's counting.)

FRANCISCO/TAK—

It was there. We needs must hie ass to young Hamlet with the 411.

HORATIO/OMAR—

Soft. I beg you film an hour more. If the camera sees nothing, neither do I.

(Mary and Tak try to find something to save the scene but no one speaks and we are left to wait on the ocean to provide a monster.)

———

It sounds funny now, but we're down here, a thousand feet beneath the Atlantic, because we wanted to see a squid. Archteuthis, thirty feet long with a bite that can take your hand off. Almost all of what the world knows about the creature has been discovered by our old man. Studies based on squid parts that came in with the tide and undigested beaks in the bellies of sperm whales.

The thing our professor knows best has eluded him all of his life.

No one has seen Archteuthis in the wild.

"So where does that leave us?" he asks. He twists a pencil into one of his eyebrows. "Without a father's ghost, what happens to Hamlet?"

"The happy version?"

"Nah," Tak says. "Kid's still screwed. That first monologue, his too, too solid flesh or whatever. He's talking unweeded gardens before he knows boo about any ghost. No pun."

"None taken," says Mary.

"I always think Pappy Hamlet is clumsy anyway," Tak says. "Ooo, I'm dead. Ooo, I'm scary."

"Frankly," Omar says, "the whole thing is pretty stupid. Four hours about a guy making a decision. Fucking to be or not to be."

We look at him and wait for the old man to answer.

"The first time I was sent to tag whales, in the Pacific," he says. "Nothing for days. I spent the whole time deciding whether to turn back."

I watch Mary. She is still wearing her costume from the first scene, a mechanical pair of overalls with a French company name sewn on the front pocket. It was all we could find. Our Denmark is a Canadian sub, a giant maple leaf painted on her nose. The uniform is too big and she looks boyish. For some reason, with her looking nothing like she should, it is easier to think about our life in London. She catches me and bites her thumb.

"Do you bite your thumb at me?"

"I do bite my thumb, sir, but not at you."

"See," says Tak, "This flirting stuff. It's no fun for us. Unless you plan on biting each other's thumbs, save it."

"That's not our speed," I say.

"We cuddle," she says. "And he sometimes winks chastely into the azure blue of my blah, blah, blah."

"I'll take it," Tak says.

Tak can't be a minister. I find it improbable, not because of his candor but because of his age. There are facts he is eager to disclose. He was born in Seoul, raised in Nova Scotia, educated in the States. His adopted parents are Icelandic. Blonde as the sun, he says. He admits to having a degree in English and marine biology, a master's in mechanical engineering. There hardly seems time for Jesus.

He checks our instruments again. He crosses himself and mumbles.

"Whatever works," he says when he realizes I was watching.

It was Tak who first noticed our propeller wasn't responding. He was making progress on fixing it when we lost our radio and sonar. He was good to explain it so that I could understand. The propeller was mechanical, possible to fix until, without navigation, we had imbedded ourselves in the ocean floor. He didn't think we had sunk so deep.

The communications failure is probably sediment. Something thick, he said, messing up our sound. Some kind of cloud we didn't pick up until we were in it. Whatever is fuzzing us out, he said, will fuzz anybody they send after us. A couple miles of static at least. They know we're out here, he said, but finding us will be a trick.

Our odds of seeing Archteuthis were never good, no better than parachuting into a random spot in North America to see a Grizzly Bear. We had a couple of leads and were able to track a group of diving whales before the sub stopped cooperating.

"Shall we continue," says the old man.

I have never heard him talk of the squid, not directly. Everything I know of his obsession is secondhand, no more immediate than listening to my father describe a Jefferson Airplane live show.

"There's got to be," Omar says, "something better to do."

"The story's started."

"*Hamlet*'s not the story," Omar says. "If you're after evidence, just hit record."

"I've never cared much for evidence," says the old man. "Accountants use evidence. We are in the business of documentation."

"Same thing."

"I don't think so," he says. "But we can stop."

"Screw that," Tak says. "I'm just getting the hang of this Francisco."

"He won't be in the rest of the play," I tell him.

"I'll get the hang of somebody else."

"This," Omar says. "It's not mine."

No one answers.

Tak and Mary start to dress the set.

With the outside spots still on — empty and dense light coming through the portals — it is easy to forget there is anything outside. A few feet is the whole world. It is a feeling I have known before and forgotten. Riding in the back seat through blizzards while my father had his brights on, it was possible to imagine that I had never really stolen candy bars with Timothy Vargus or tried to hold hands with Allison Saunders by the tornado slide. The feeling didn't make the possibility of a ditch and freezing to death any less scary. But it was exhilarating. Rationing a bottle of water between my knees, I wanted those trips to last as long as the bag of licorice I was sharing with my sister.

———

Scene II. — Elsinore. A Room of State in the Castle

(I shoot low-angle from beneath the sub's instruments, my back to the Ocean. I am cramped but think I can get through it. I wanted a shot that would include some of our screens and gadgetry. And we needed a wall to hang a few of our maps on.)

CLAUDIUS/OMAR—

(We made a crown from pie plates and electrical tape. Tak had several pieces of jewelry in a tackle box. For luck, he said. Carries them every-where. We have affixed them, watches and rings and pendants, to a long skirt of Mary's. As Tak dresses him, Omar is not cooperating so much as standing still. He reads from the old man's notes and scratches his face. He decides to improvise.)

According to this, our brother's dead. I'm sure you all know that. Good King Hamlet. Poor King Hamlet. Dead King Ham-let. His widow and all.

He's dead. I'm not. Your queen has remarried. If I were to die, I would my wife had found such happiness.

POLONIUS/TAK—

Baby, we know all that. You the king now. What's the hoo-ha?

(Tak is wearing a shirt that says Old Fart, Pull finger. He looks di-rectly into the camera.)

That's iambic right? Hoo-ha?

(Looks at Claudius/Omar)

It's the circumstance of your wedding that doth provoke this interest.

CLAUDIUS/OMAR—

You don't know anything about my circumstance.

POLONIUS/TAK—

(He is quiet for a while, finally makes a decision. He raises his eyebrows. I've never seen him pick a fight. He is good at everything.)

I listen better than you think.

(Omar is looking at him. Tak's voice gets sharper.)

She was pregnant. Six months if my math holds. You were both too young, but she's stayed a better queen than you've played king.

CLAUDIUS/OMAR—

(He hits Tak hard in the face.

Tak spits blood. I zoom to his mouth.

Omar is angry but he seems emptied, his tall body sagging. He turns to the camera. I think he is deciding whether to speak directly to his wife. He waits too long to say anything important, begins to read again.)

It is as you say, most gracious Polonius.
But now, my cousin Hamlet, and my son, how is it that the
clouds still hang on you?

HAMLET/OLD MAN—

*(He is all in black, shorts and a T-shirt. Without sleeves, you can see
the age spots on his arms but he has them folded defiantly. We have,
with blue marker, drawn hair on his head. Mary thought it disre-
spectful but it was the old man's idea.)*

Not so, my lord; I am too much i'the sun. And it's all right, it's
alright.

GERTRUDE/MARY—

*(Tak wanted the part but she wouldn't hear of it. You ain't got the
corner on smut, she said. She is in a sports' bra and black jeans.)*

Good Hamlet,

(She looks at the old man the way they all do, with reverence.)

cast thy nighted color off, and let thine eye look like a friend
upon our Denmark.

Do not forever seek for thy losses in the dust. Thou know'st
'Tis common. All that live must cease — and in their ceasing,
dear Prince, thou must not cease, but regard the world anew
with pleasing humor and sweetened breath.

HAMLET/OLD MAN—

And in times of trouble, my mother Mary came to me.

GERTRUDE/MARY—

If it be so, why seems it so particular with thee?

HAMLET/OLD MAN—

Seems, madam! Nay, it is. I know not seems.

(I think he is searching for a line. He gives up.)

I met Picasso on the street while I was in college. He seemed dull, a coward. I gave him a textbook and a grease pen. On the back cover, below the periodic table, he drew me perfectly, as I ugly as I was.

Appearance doth not smack of anything. I will not speak of seems.

POLONIUS/TAK—

(He approaches the camera, kneels in front of me.)

Ray-Ray. While we're talking about seems. You look real good in that car, right? I know, baby. But you don't like being a lawyer. I know this is gonna piss you off. But you're lucky. No one, these days, gets a dead brother telling them to change jobs.

(Tak stands again and changes his mind. He comes back to me. As he speaks, Omar takes off his crown and leaves the control room. Exeunt or whatever.)

If I start talking to the rest of you, I won't stop. And we've got a play to do. Forgive me, alright?

(He returns to the scene. He notices Omar is gone but continues talking to the old man.)

O tut. Thou art no more or less miserable than anyone.
This death of ours, 'tis the theme of all.

Tut. Tut. But list. 'Tis natural. Like your mamma says. For your father lost a father, and your father lost, lost his. And Joseph begot Esau. And both are fathers lost who lost fathers.

It's all one. And beside the point. If not for other causes, I believe you would dash your obsequious sorrow to the ground, strip the black from your bones and dance in your regal buff.

HAMLET/OLD MAN—

And tell me what thou, an ancient man of thirty years, can know of mine other causes.

POLONIUS/TAK—

Baby, I gots eyes.
Your mamma's half-naked, sleeping with your uncle. If I were thou, t'would be enough for me to persevere in obstinate condolement.

HAMLET/OLD MAN—

Well said, dawg-P.

POLONIUS/TAK—

Actually, noble prince, 'tis P-dawg that doth adorn the lips of
yon homeys that do but call me by that name.

GERTRUDE/MARY—

So anyway. The king is gone and we must follow. Let not thy
mother lose her prayers, Hamlet.

*(Exeunt all but Hamlet. He picks up the charts, fiddles a moment with
our bum radio.)*

HAMLET/OLD MAN—

Every time this story has happened,
Broadway or wherever, I have been left
alone to long for death. Again it is true
this time. I am sick of living. I am,
as any Hamlet before me, in black
to mourn my father's sins. There was a time,
I was seven, in Austria between
the wars. My father — he was a man, no
better — gave me an English bible. He
spoke the language when he argued. For love
he used another. He said the book would
give answers if I had questions. It

took four years to finish. I still
had not been to church, save cathedrals we
visited like museums. My questions
were given sun and water. I read
other books in other languages. If
he had told me the truth, what it means
not to know, I would have been a better
lover, a better father. I would have
sold fish in a city of constant rain.
I would not have taken these children to
the bottom of the world to die. There are
others I have done worse to. Rosencrantz
and Guildenstern should have known me better.

*(He has two daughters, both musicians. One a pop star in Europe, the
other in a philharmonic somewhere. He, Mary said, brags about hiding their chemistry books so they had no distractions. She said it was
that they would not respect him, see him like a black sheep uncle, something to work away from. He watches them via press dispatches and
liner notes from their albums.)*

O, that this too, too solid flesh would melt,
thaw, resolve itself into a dew. Or
that the Everlasting had not fixed his
cannon 'gainst self-slaughter. And yet, 'tis far
too late for this Hamlet. If, as Hamlets
have so proclaimed, undiscovered country
doth await my frail frame, I should have, with
my wife, set sail from this unkindly place
long ere now. Stale, flat, and unprofitable
do seem all the uses of this world. Alas,
the path my wife took hence from this un-weeded

garden hath grown over, as hard to trace
as ink in water. 'Tis neither sin nor dreams
that doth keep this Hamlet breathing. I would
set forth now if not so encumbered
by four who would be better served to stay.
So, like any Hamlet worth his madness,
I will wait too long, speak in rhyme as we,
like poison in a glass of wine, dissolve.

————

When we figure out that he has finished, Mary helps him sit down.

"Methinks," she says, "the professor doth protest too much."

The old man is crying.

Tak speaks.

"I get the next monologue," he says. "I won't screw off, I promise."

"Sure," the old man says. I see that his hands are curled and shaking, the color of unprocessed sugar. He, now, is less our leader than our most important talisman, a diploma or grade school track ribbon that must be pampered with acid free paper. "We can all be Hamlet down here."

"O," Mary says, "my dreams may of yet be delivered."

She says it funny, Shakespeare's stressed syllables, but no one laughs.

"How much air?" the Professor asks.

"Five hours," says Tak. "Four good ones."

Underwater, silence is never silent. Things drip and echo.

"Look at this," Tak says. "I wasn't gonna spill it. But look. We've got ten more meters of sonar then we had an hour ago. Which gives us a total of ten." He tries to laugh. "Whatever it is, it's clearing. Slowly. We will be found. It's a matter of when."

Mary squeezes my earlobe. I smile at her and she squeezes it harder.

Tak is looking at his instruments. I can tell he is frustrated by how slowly they change, frustrated that he knows the answers are not good ones, frustrated that he can't stop checking.

"Hurry," says the old man. "Our Hamlets must meet their ghosts." For a moment he is not arthritic. He stands and begins to remove his clothing. "You will need these," he says to Tak. He is naked but his underwear. There is something beautiful about his body.

To stop staring, I leave to find Omar.

He is on one of the bunks, sitting the way Mary was sitting behind me. He holds a book open on his lap and rocks autistic.

"What are you reading?"

"Words, words, words," he says.

"We need Horatio."

"Words."

"Are you game?"

He stops moving and looks at me.

"She was the right woman," he says. "It's easy to forget."

"None of my business."

"Right. You need a Horatio."

He leaves the book open, on the abandoned bunk. It is a diagnostic manual for some of our equipment, charts and symbols, numbers that spread and twist across the page.

———

(We decide to pick the scene up were we left off. I don't care if anyone notices a different Hamlet. We barely have a plot now.)

HORATIO/OMAR—

Sweet Prince.

HAMLET/TAK—

(The garments worn by the old man are too tight on Tak. They make him look in poor taste, like me at the gym ready for a game of racquet-ball.)

H-Dawg. 'Tis Horatio, is it not?

HORATIO/OMAR—

The same.

HAMLET/TAK—

We'll teach you to drink deep 'ere you leave.

HORATIO/OMAR—

I doubt it not, my lord, for what I think I've seen.

(He is steady with his lines. He's still not acting per se, but at least he's not being obstinate.)

HAMLET/TAK—

And I doubt not your not doubting. For, as is known the world o'er, 'tis much to be seen and more to be drunk in the deeps of this great country. I could, if you would have me, give some kickass recitation about our stacks of canned tuna. Jars of cheese whiz. More bottled water than your aunt Helga needs.

HORATIO/OMAR—

'Tis none of those things.

HAMLET/TAK—

But none? We're talking stacks of tuna. Stacks.

HORATIO/OMAR—

In deference, sweet wag, thou wert always such a smart prince.
Thou would do thyself some good to list.
I may have seen a man who looked much like the king, thy father.

HAMLET/TAK—

As have I. There was this one Halloween, kook dressed up like a cat. O Grrrrtrude.

HORATIO/OMAR—

But lord, last night. I perhaps did see him on the rampart.

HAMLET/TAK—

Floor's yours.

HORATIO/OMAR—

In the dead vast and middle of the night did I, upon hearing such reports, take it upon my stead to brave the cruel —

HAMLET/TAK—

Forget it.

HORATIO/OMAR—

But—

HAMLET/TAK—

I said 'twas no matter.

HORATIO/OMAR—

But 'tis the matter, the very heart.

HAMLET/TAK—

Nay.

HORATIO/OMAR—

Fuck it. If he's not going to go ahead with this. Fuck it.

(Exeunt Omar. Tak crawls to my camera, his face close to the lens. He is manic and strange.)

HAMLET/TAK—

Do not worry, dear hearts, I shall be brief.
When I was little, I timed my preacher
as he spoke. I don't remember what was
so important. fly fishing on TV?
Pro wrestling? Hard to say. Nonetheless,
I wanted to know exactly how much
breath the codger spent. I did not use
the timer, but with the calculator
did add one plus one plus one until I
had compiled ten minutes worth of seconds.
I wanted to be part of time. Ritalin
made me less jumpy and I left the watch
at home. God was easier to hear
without the hour. If my father
wanders the night, things will fall apart
without me talking to him. Just a sec.

*(He gets up to leave. He returns with a golf club. Hamlet begins to
smash our instruments. Omar enters and tries to stop him but is too
late.)*

I will not talk to my Father. If death
is the script, t'will be a tart surprise. And
prais'd be rashness, for it should remind
me there's a divinity that shapes our ends,
rough-hew them how we will.

*(I have not stopped filming, even as I was covered with shards of plas-
tic and glass. Tak nods to me and I shut off the camera.)*

———

"There is more to Heaven and to Earth," Tak says to Omar, "Than is dreamt of in all of your philosophy, Horatio."

"Fucking shit," Omar says. He quiets.

Tak gives us nothing.

The old man begins to write again.

Mary finds me and offers to pull me up. She smiles. I tug at her and she falls to me.

Tak sits with the old man.

Mary and I are kissing, frantic but nothing sloppy.

Omar cries loudly, near our feet.

His kids are little, nine and seven, I think. His wife decorates cakes. Mary told me his kids can't go to church, not even after a sleep-over. And, she said, he taught them to hunt and fish, to take care of themselves if the house should burn or he and his wife were to find themselves in a plane crash.

He is a choking mess, snot on his shirt, eyes swollen.

Eventually Mary escapes our kisses and gets me to my feet. She leads me to the sleeping quarters where, at last, our final hours resemble something worthy of a promise.

———

Scene III. — Elsinore. A public room.

(When Mary and I return to the front, Omar has composed himself. Tak and the old man have us write down every line we can remember.

I am fairly certain that most of our memories are not from Hamlet. *Without a ghost, we have only Claudius and Polonius talking. I suggest that, to move the play along, Ophelia could bring news of the murder in the garden.*

The professor said he was finally ready to play an old man.)

POLONIUS/OLD MAN—

I think — or else my brain has turned to mush, an octopus's garden in the shade, if you will — that I have found the very cause of Hamlet's lunacy.

CLAUDIUS/OMAR—

(He is back in the adorned skirt.)

O, speak of that. Why would he turn our kingdom to rubble?

POLONIUS/OLD MAN—

My liege, all he needs is love. Love. Love is all he needs.

CLAUDIUS/OMAR—

Peace, you mumbling fool!

POLONIUS/OLD MAN—

I speak but true. For he has been seen in my house of late. With love's light wings did he o'er-perch my walls; for stony limits cannot hold love out.
I have ta'en from my daughter this.

(He reads. Mary wrote the letter. She gets to be Hamlet next.)

Sweet baby and your great big chest—
That's an ill phrase, great big is a vile phrase: but you shall hear.
— Doubt that fish have gills, a lobster claws, the movies lights and lawyers flaws, but do not doubt that your hips are hot enough to pop peanuts from their shells. Or that I will lick the salt right up.
Right up forever.
Hamlet.

CLAUDIUS/OMAR—

That's awful. Does she love him?

POLONIUS/OLD MAN—

I think so.

CLAUDIUS/OMAR—

If it's mutual, how be he mad?

POLONIUS/OLD MAN—

There is no woman's sides can bide the beating of so strong a passion as the love that beats his heart: no woman's heart so big to hold so much; they lack retention. Alas, their love may be called appetite, — no motion of the liver, but the palate, — where his is all as hungry as the sea. Therein, he is mad. He loves her, yeah, yeah, yeah.

CLAUDIUS/OMAR—

I would I could take your word.

POLONIUS/OLD MAN—

(There is an awkward moment as he gestures for Mary to enter.)

Here comes the lover now. Do but mark the nature of his madness.

HAMLET/MARY—

(On her, the Hamlet black looks more nautical than sad. Tak wanted her to have a skull. All we've got is a rubber version of Archteuthis.)

To be, or not to be, — that is the question; —
But it's not the right one. I've never liked
it. Suicide seems so stupid. Maybe
not in principle, but for him. Even if —
as is custom by the time Hamlet
speaks these lines — he knows his
uncle killed his father, it seems to me
a reason for a lawyer, not
self slaughter. O big bad uncle! I'll show
you! By killing mine self. 'Tis a madness
indeed. And of his mom — I guess
she's my mom now — let me talk about my mom.
She didn't even wait for my father
to die, let alone funeral meats or
whatever, before she was in Cleveland
with an ass of man. Every time I tried to talk,

she said I just didn't like change, or it was
because Bert wasn't British that I hated
him. Never mind Champ being a Yankee.
It's true I was pissed. But never did I
take up arms against a sea of trouble.

(She pauses. She is looking at me. And then at the camera.)

Mother. I will not claim understanding.
But what you've done doth not linger pressing
on my heart. All I will say is talk to dad,
or anyone, for methinks your memory's wrong.
You suffered no slings and arrows, knew no
outrageous fortune. But you will do what you will.

(We were married the summer her parents split.

*We honeymooned in small towns in Minnesota. She had never been to
the middle states and wanted to eat at the places I ate at as a child. She
let me choose for her, spent ten days eating chicken-fried steak and
biscuits and gravy. Waitresses made her order two or three times
because they liked how she talked.*

*There are no photos of us on the trip. None of her because she wouldn't
let me. And she didn't want any of me by myself. If you die first, she
said, I wouldn't be able to do anything but look at you. So we took
pictures of empty fields and buildings.)*

Anyhow, I do not understand Hamlet
and the whole Ophelia thing. She's hot.
If I love her, as I just told her I do,
why don't I ask her for help. Or better

yet, why not just hole up with her. To sleep —
to sleep with her, — perchance to dream: ay, there's
the rub, the thousand natural shocks the flesh
is heir to. I mean sex is not everything,
but sometimes it should be. For this Hamlet
it is. Ophelia. Nymph. O
in thy orisons, be all my sins remembered.
Ophelia, I would I could feel ya.
But soft, she comes. But soft. She comes. She comes.

OPHELIA/TAK—

(His drag is tasteful, no fake boobs. Just a jumper of Mary's and a festive, summer hat. His voice finds a sultry note I didn't know him capable of.)

My lord, I have remembrances of you.

HAMLET/MARY—

Deliver away, goddess.

OPHELIA/TAK—

But soft, dear heart.

(I close the shot to Mary's face alone. I know he is supposed to tell her about the uncle conspiracy, but I am hoping Tak will give words to what I cannot. I want proof of her love, even if it is transplanted.)

I have no idea what to say. It was something about your parents' bed.

HAMLET/MARY—

(Strangely, I am getting what I wanted. She looks at him the way she did when I ruined my first load of mutual laundry.)

'Tis not the bed of Denmark that does concern me. If you would follow me, I would we quit this place and end our play in marriage.

OPHELIA/TAK—

O.

HAMLET/MARY—

I would you would.

OPHELIA/TAK—

Why?

HAMLET/MARY—

Madness. Love. Your hips in that outfit. A fair thought to lie between maids' legs.

OPHELIA/TAK—

O.

HAMLET/MARY—

Hie thee, with me, to a nunnery where thou may prove a breeder of sinners.

OPHELIA/TAK—

O.

HAMLET/MARY—

If we stay here, we shall have a plague for a dowry — if thou needs must marry, and I totally hope thou doth — marry this fool.

OPHELIA/TAK—

(He finally stops gawking and begins to laugh. He is having a hard time standing.)

O. It is most like. Whiplash. We could instead, as I am not supposed to. Not supposed too, shhhh. Mary. We could whip-lash right now.

HAMLET/MARY—

Soft, soft.

OPHELIA/TAK—

Nonny, nonny.

(He is breathing weird.)

Nay, nay. I need sturdier stuff. Swear not by the moon.

(He sings.)

For you are dead and gone, lady, you are dead and gone, at your
head a grass green turf, at your heels a stone.
They say the whale was the baker's daughter. O

HAMLET/MARY—

O.

(I am thinking about sperm whales, gray bricks the size of buses.)

O. O. O. I know. Invite them to supper. Let's invite our king
and queen to supper. You can make Cornish game hens.

OLD MAN—

*(Where'd he come from? He was watching and now he's in the scene.
O. 'Tis mysterious strange. He is laughing too. Who's he supposed to
be?)*

We'd love to. Supper. We'd love to.

HAMLET/MARY—

Sure. Come to supper. You bet.

(Sperm whales sleep upside down. No one knows why. Or how. No one knew they even did it until a year ago. Or so. Mary said. For a while she had God because of whales. Whales who eat squid. Monsters who eat monsters. Mary said she had God. A god of monsters and what we don't know. We know they make sound, sound that bounces, Mary said, off their skull and out. We know it bounces out. Maybe sonar, maybe song, maybe directions to other monsters. We don't know, Mary said. We know they have a big gland in their head, something like oil. She and Tak and Omar and the old man saw them sleep. Upside down, she said. They all do it. Go from straight to tipped, their big flat noses pointed down. Down. She showed me the tape, a different camera man. Maybe prettier than me. God in whales, tipping at the same time, from straight to down. All of them upside down. Beneath the swell and undertow, undisturbed, perfect upside-down.)

———

Scene IV. — The Submarine.

(Out of character but breathing now. The canisters of air the old man brought for his cancer. We all have them, enough to go around and one more.

My head has cleared slightly. I have a headache but am able to focus. I would stop recording but I don't see the point. I crawl to Mary and put her head in my lap.

We have to take our air pieces off to speak. Omar says he hasn't been Hamlet yet. I didn't get a soliloquy, he says. The old man agrees that it's his turn. In a sec, Mary says. The old man asks where we are. Hamlet, I say, just invited his parents to supper. Right-o, Mary says. What are the rules, Omar asks. Tell the truth, the old man says.

It occurs to me that I will be the only one without a Hamlet in the mix, without some control of the story. And Omar would not be my choice to end. But no one else can work the camera. So they claim. But soft.)

———

Scene V. — Elsinore. A dining room.

(The floor of the only room we've been in. We clean it up.)

HAMLET/OMAR—

(He doesn't bother with the costume. He is crying again.)

I can no longer, i'faith, hold my peace. I
would have here ta'en my objection with me
silent. Not now. You saw. We could not breathe,
our bodies frothing like crazed cattle.
By my troth, or whatever, this is not right.
Air must expire, that I understand.
But to use so much wind on a movie
of a play of a story we can
scarce remember; 'tis an occasion that doth
inform against me and spur me to revenge.

*(His line smacks of the original. I don't know where the words come
from. Perhaps he has known it all along. Perhaps this is what the old
man meant earlier, when he said we would find what we needed to.
Perhaps we should have done a musical.)*

But now, it is over. We did nothing
to prolong our lives and so end them. Yet
I live to say, This thing's to do; I still
have cause, and will, and strength, and means, and air
to do something. O, from this time forth, let
my thoughts be bloody, or be nothing worth!

OPHELIA/MARY—

(I don't know if he's finished but she's brought the others to interrupt him. Probably a good idea.

Claudius and Gertrude enter. The old man struggles with his oxygen tank, the little golf cart caddie tipping on one wheel.

It seems that their roles are finally correct.)

Do we forget ourselves or do we have dinner plans? The Cornish game hens are dry but who cares.

HAMLET/OMAR—

This thing's to do.

OPHELIA/MARY—

And then it's straight to Friar Lawrence, yes? You haven't changed your mind, have you dear sweet?

HAMLET/OMAR—

Not a whit.

Mother. Uncle. Leave the wringing of your hands. Peace; sit you down and let me wring your hearts, for so I shall if they be made of penetrable stuff.

GERTRUDE/TAK—

What I have I done, that thou dar'st wag thy tongue in noise
so rude against me?

HAMLET/OMAR—

Such an act that blurs the grace and blush of modesty, calls
virtue hypocrite, takes the rose from the fair forehead of inno-
cence and sets a blister there; O, such a deed. To turn our last
hours into this.

Look thee upon this picture—

(He digs for his wallet)

Here is my wife. Ha! Have you eyes?

CLAUDIUS/OLD MAN—

'Tis my offense that is rank. I should have come alone.

GERTRUDE/TAK—

My lord, t'was not you that did damn us.

HAMLET/OMAR—

But ere we started, this king was already dead. O villainy!

(He uses his metal oxygen tank to beat our old man. The professor falls immediately and tries to speak.)

Here thou murderous, damned Dane.

(As it is happens, I don't move. Tak uses his own tank as a club. He hits Omar in the shoulder.)

GERTRUDE/TAK—

A hit. A very palpable hit.

(Omar is quick, able to knock Tak off of his feet. He, with both hands, brings his canister down on Tak's head several times.

I watch Mary attack Omar from behind. She hits him with the sharp end of the tank, once, hard enough to knock her valve loose. Omar, Tak, and the Old Man are unconscious.

My wife's air is hissing.)

OPHELIA/MARY—

Horatio.

(I assume she is already hallucinating when I realize she is talking to me. I bring her the spare canister.)

No. I am dead. Give me yours and take the fresh one.

HORATIO/ME—

You get the fresh one.

OPHELIA/MARY—

Give me your air, Horatio. List. Enough.
Listen, Champ. You promised.

(If it couldn't be together, she would go first.

I am aware of how poorly-written our final moments will seem to whatever Fortinbras reclaims our Denmark, but I do not look for words.

I wrap the camera in plastic and keep it running. The tape will either make a few newscasts and disappear, or it will make it to video stores and be shown at teenage slumber parties. Or perhaps it is Archteuthis that is our Fortinbras, and this story will live a mile under water.

I retrieve the fresh tank and give mine to Mary.

She is dying slightly faster than I am.

We sit, facing each other with our masks on. Our knees touch. I hold her hand and take her pulse. She slumps against a bulkhead. I can't see her mouth. I lean closer.

This is how we sit when the power dies.

When it comes to it, I will do what she wants but won't say. I will stay alive. I will seek air from the others, from the dead. And through our large portal — the ocean teeming with life and secrets but no light — I will keep watch.)

❧ The Seventeenth Aureliano and Jesus (Who Was Thirteen in Number) ❧

When the man who had been Scott Mueller mentioned his father — a man more important than fire — the doctors assumed that he was referring to one Yahweh or another. During his interview, they clicked their tongues so that the Seventeenth Son of the colonel began to suspect that they did not believe him. He told them of the book that would explain everything. "It's all written down," he said, though he could not provide them with a title and the doctors never asked, thinking that they already knew.

The man who was not Scott Mueller still did not trust these doctors without instruments, but he was relieved that they were finally listening to him, taking extensive notes as he spoke of his book and his father. With their act of writing, he was committed and moved into the hospital wing that housed the thirteen incarnations of Christ.

Even after he had been living there for some time, the seventeenth Aureliano was afraid to remember which Saint the building was named for. If the subject was brought up he would squelch it much in the way his father had stifled similar talk while leading his 37 revolutions against the conservatives. "The saints," they both said, "only get people in trouble."

On the day he remembered that he was to die, the seventeenth son of the Colonel was not allowed any other memory. It was often the case with his family that, in their last moments, time would unfurl like a great sponge torn open and spread out. On its newly revealed surface, the dying would find unexpected minutes to scour whichever events of the past he or she would choose. If the pen that had interrupted death so many times for his family would have intervened, he might have used his memory to count the sixteen brothers killed before him. He might have tasted fried bananas in the well-swept kitchen of his grandmother Ûrsula. He might have listened to the ripe fullness of a tin roof battered by Macondo's rain, or remembered his grandfather describing the weather as a miserable sickness that stops for no one, not even the dead.

On the day he was to finish living, however, there was no intervention, and he was not allowed to dwell on anything, not even the morning he hadn't been related to the Colonel but was simply a carpenter, reading.

His daughter had left the book when she returned to school a few weeks before. In those days, when he was Scott Mueller, he had grown fond of reading on the balcony where he smoked after-work cigars, aged carefully in the humidor that had been one of his first carpentry projects. That morning, he experienced the horrible deaths of the Colonel's first sons, sixteen young men marked with ashen crosses on their foreheads. The first Aurelianos were hunted down in a single chapter while his brother Timothy drove the Mueller and Sons' truck. The murders were enough to pick the book up again when he and his brother had finished mitering a door frame and decided to take their lunch in the bed of the pickup before clouds could blow in.

It was then, while his brother poured soup from a Thermos, that Scott Mueller read the two hundred and forty-sixth page. Even before he finished, he began to make a noise, a sound his brother would latter swear identical to the shriek a lizard makes when it squirts its own blood. On the page, the seventeenth

Aureliano "eluded his executioners and leapt over the courtyard wall to lose himself in the labyrinth of the world." By the time the last son of the Colonel finished reading that he himself "was never heard from again," Scott Mueller had stopped making noise.

When leaping over the courtyard wall, he had not expected to see such houses on the other side, painted in brilliant hues that wouldn't last a single rainy season. He had planned on hiding in the mountains because he knew them like the back of his hand, having been partially raised by Indians. As he re-read page 246 he discovered that his plans were written out exactly. "But this," he said as he dropped the book to look at a man he didn't know, "this will not do." He watched trees that lined the street shake with the breeze and discovered that several of them had needles where he would have expected leaves. "I don't think I like this place," he said and he didn't change his mind until he no longer had to look at the city.

And so, on the day the seventeenth Aureliano stumbled over the courtyard wall, he looked upon the world as one born against his will. Because he could not fully comprehend the gravity of his newness without a mirror to show the light, freckled skin around his eyes where his face had so recently been dark and wrinkled, he could only think about the strangeness of the corridor of new houses.

"If there is a God," he said, "I won't last long now."

When he ran his hand through his hair, the seventeenth Aureliano was startled by the way it twisted and caught at his fingers. Long when he went over the wall, it was now scratchy, tight, and close to the scalp, the hair that earned Scott Mueller the schoolboy nicknames of Wooly and Sheeps. He grunted and spat the way he had seen his father, the Colonel, spit on the dusty workshop floor when the aging man retired, once again, to make golden fishes. He decided, as Timothy watched him, that the only way to deal with people who thought they knew him was to let them.

"People will think what they goddamned will," he would have said if he were alone. Out of fear, he promised himself to say as little as possible and to eventually find a quiet room with a door he could lock. But, despite his name, he had never resembled the Aurelianos in the family, and the truth of his nature would make his father's solitude impossible for him. So too did his hair, as soon as he unwound his hand from it, begin to straighten and darken until it was as black as it had ever been in Macondo.

It would continue to grow at a monstrous rate until several months after he was dead.

————

On the day that Scott Mueller read page 246, his grandmother, who was also named Ursula, found a hundred lizards. She found them every place, in her cupboards, under the plumbing in the bathroom, sprawled on the hot shingles outside of her windows. By the time Scott Mueller's wife and brother had tired of the seventeenth Aureliano, Ursula could, even when she was sleeping, hear the lizards scrabbling on the roof, scratching inside her walls, hissing and feeding.

Eventually, she decided to use the telephone for help but could only reach the Mueller's voice mail. When Sarah and Timothy Mueller returned to the house after leaving the seventeenth son of the Colonel at the hospital, there were no messages. The answering system did not consider the message worth remembering until all involved were dead and it would play at random, shaking the entire house with her amplified voice.

In order to get the seventeenth Aureliano to the hospital, Scott Mueller's wife and brother told him they were finally going to visit the sea he had often described as the "only remedy for the symptoms of this city." He believed them and sat quietly in the truck amongst his suitcases. "This is not the sea," he said when they arrived at the building, its gargoyles leering like landed fish. "It seems one never gets where one is going." And with that, the seventeenth son of the Colonel began to trot up the oversized steps, carrying his own bags, whistling a ballad that no one could recognize.

The weeks before had not been easy for the Muellers. Because he could not keep his promise of solitude, the seventeenth Aureliano had not sought isolation and had, in fact, became vain about continuing the daily affairs of his predecessor, though very few of those tasks made any sense to him. On the days Timothy Mueller sat buckled into the passenger's seat, expecting him to drive, the seventeenth Aureliano could not bring himself to admit he did not understand the machine. He, whomever he was supposed to be, was still the son of a Colonel great enough to serve God roasted meat balanced on the boots he wore to war. So, as his father and grandfather had done with gadgets the Gypsies brought to Macondo, he simply made do. He pushed the vehicle as fast as he could make it go, turning corners several blocks after Timothy told him to. Often he turned for no reason at all, as if he had simply grown suspicious of their direction.

"He is not going crazy," Timothy told Sara in private. "Is it possible to go stupid?"

Luckily for everyone involved, the seventeenth Aureliano had been a carpenter in Macondo and things smoothed out at the job site. He knew how to sand and miter, how to router and stain. Though it took a few days to stop looking for manual tools, he was skilled enough that he only needed to scorch the wood once or twice before mastering their electric versions.

For several weeks, everything was mostly the same as it had

been but done differently. He never mentioned anything about Macondo or his father, and the family acted as if Scott Mueller had simply caught a very confusing cold. Their impressions changed when the seventeenth Aureliano, while smoking a cigar on the balcony, tossed Scott Mueller's humidor into the street. When asked, he replied, "If I am stuck in this place, I will smoke how I smoke. And that goes for everything."

And so it did, especially when he approached Sara in the bedroom that night. Because he was as blessed as the José Arcadios of the family, he had never been bothered by the awkward fumblings that plagued the other Aurelianos. He clutched her ankles and lifted her as though she was no more cumbersome than a sawhorse. Her reluctance left her when she hit the bed. His hair was not his only part to resume the form he had been accustomed to in Macondo. When he removed his clothing, he descended to her exactly as God had made him. Between the biting and licking, the unnatural sounds and cruel tickles, the seventeenth Aureliano had no trouble distracting her from the resolute cross composed of ash that she had been unable to scrub from her husband's forehead. Coital hours mounted like a catalogue of forgotten animals and she waited for days, each night kindled with a fire of several flames, before she asked about their new habits.

The seventeenth Aureliano said only, "I am the son of a great Colonel."

When she laughed as though he had removed his underclothes to reveal a potted begonia between his thighs, he became indignant and boastful, telling the stories of his family, from his grandparents' arrival in Macondo to his departure, without stopping for breath. She decided right then and there that he had gone mad, though she gave herself several more nights before she let her brother-in law convince her to do anything about it.

At first, Sara tried to listen to the stories as one would a new, strange laugh or some other charming attempt at spontaneity. At that time, however, the seventeenth Aureliano still had most of his memories from Macondo, and she was unable to find the stammers or contradictions that should have plagued the tales if they were invented for romance. Nonetheless, she let herself believe — especially in the evenings and sometimes after he returned from work smelling of sawdust and varnish to envelope her even before his cigar — that she could go on indefinitely.

As she read magazines next to Timothy in the waiting room, she cared less that the doctors could fix her husband than she hoped they would let her take him home. When this did not happen and the doctors suggested he would only recover with long-term care, she became withdrawn and eventually — because her visits only allowed speaking privileges — left the city. She worked in a reptile emporium and spent her nights writing the stories her husband had told her. She discovered she was pregnant and stayed that way until she finished recording what she knew of the history of Macondo.

Upon completion of the manuscript, some four years after it had been started, she finally gave birth to a boy who, like every Aureliano, was received with his eyes open.

On the day Ursula Mueller tried the telephone, Timothy Mueller had stopped answering the phone in order to work without sleep, running his saws all through the night with the help of a string of assistants who kept quitting because of his tyrannical hours and an insistence that he call them Scott or Sheeps. In fact, Timothy Mueller did nothing but speak fondly of his brother whenever he was not cutting or building, which was not very often. He would continue to work tirelessly until some years later his body simply fell dead of exhaustion.

Without an answer from anyone, Ursula Mueller eventually had no choice but to take a broom of her own onto the roof. She tried to shoo away a particularly mischievous-looking lizard that had once been scared out of Ûrsula Buendia's kitchen in Macondo, a lizard that would later be found by the thirteen Christs. As she swung recklessly, she heard herself say, "time changes, but not so much." She stopped to consider what her words might have meant but lost her balance and, without understanding, fell to the ground where her body remained undiscovered for a full year. Even after she had been buried, time was not corrosive to her and her features did not change in the slightest. Her obituary ran opposite a story confirming that the plumbing within one city block of her house had been acting strangely; if one read carefully between the two articles, one might believe that her death had caused the groundwater to smell of jasmine.

———

When he learned that a bullet had perforated the cross made of ash that adorned the seventeenth Aureliano's forehead, the sixth Jesus spoke for all thirteen versions of Himself when he said, "This was not a good death for a Son of God." Every Jesus nodded though they all had agreed, since the afternoon he had arrived some months earlier, that the seventeenth Aureliano was nothing they had seen before. It was the sixth Jesus who, upon his entry, spoke for the entire ward by saying, "May God damn me if this one's not a bastard."

By the time he was seen by the thirteen Christs, the seventeenth Aureliano had lost some of the pudginess his inherited body had carried in its waist and neck. His skin was wrinkled again and, as he had done in Macondo's season without rain, he scraped it off in flakes every evening before sleep. He collected the skin in piles to serve as calendars of his lost years. His mustache had returned long enough to wax the tips in the fashion of his father.

"I hope you all prove better than saints," he said upon his arrival as every Jesus gathered around him. The twelfth Jesus, who had been an actor only two months earlier, could not suppress his eager nature and tried to impress the newcomer by performing the only miracle he knew, so that when the seventeenth Aureliano opened a suitcase it released a stream of colorful birds.

Because he had seen similar tricks from priests trying to raise money for cathedrals in Macondo, the seventeenth Aureliano did not react as the flock dove and pecked while the orderlies buzzed around the room. The thirteen Christs took his lack of reaction as proof of shared divinity and nodded their heads. Eventually, the tiny birds became silent, taking their place in the rafters.

"Father forgive me," said the third Jesus. Nothing more was said of it. As the hospital staff left the room without cleaning, the seventeenth Aureliano realized that he would have to be careful where he put his feet.

He looked at them and said, "By Christ, you all look the same." They did not recoil at his blasphemy. Instead they looked rather embarrassed. Even though several of them were women, two were black, and the ninth Jesus looked vaguely Puerto Rican, they all shared similar chins and noses. Every one of them had a full head of hair that, regardless of ethnicity, hung limply to their shoulders like the driest of moss.

For several days, the seventeenth Aureliano kept to himself. The others did not involve him when they gathered to practice miracles. He was bored, except for two hours each afternoon when, under strict supervision, he was allowed to carve reptiles from pieces of driftwood. Nurses visited him twice a day with pills that the doctors said would help him remember Scott Mueller's wife's maiden name and the details of his marriage proposal. He was sure that this was impossible. The pills succeeded in confiscating his memories of Macondo but left nothing to replace them. He began to pace as his father had during the revolutions, though he couldn't place the behavior because he had forgotten the stories and soon was unable to name the priest that had baptized him and his sixteen brothers with ash that would never come off. At night he was forced into a miniature bed with another set of pills. Several times, after waking up with dreams of firing squads, he was beaten by orderlies until he fell quiet. Though he recognized the conditions as unfavorable, he would not lead a revolt for nearly a year. Until he remembered who he was, he did not have to make decisions and was able to put his pride to sleep so that the days passed like commercials shown on the ward's black and white television.

During those weeks, the fifth Jesus, a woman who had once been a psychiatrist for the very same hospital, developed a miracle that would reveal the path to salvation. Even if they had arguments with her about the exact nature of transubstantiation or other elements of their divinity, every Jesus agreed that it was a great trick. The miracle resembled hypnosis without concentration or candles, and she had gotten to the point where she could perform it in full daylight. Though all of the Christs knew they were saved, there was a lot of time on their hands, so the fifth Jesus performed the miracle as a kind of business, trading it for articles of identical hospital clothing or miracles she could not do herself. When she offered to do the miracle for the seventeenth Aureliano, he tried to decline.

"Sometimes it is best not to know," he told her, "but I don't know why that is." So he paid her a pair of socks and, after he had been blessed, remembered the title of the book where, on his first day in the city, he had seen his story written down.

Eventually, the seventeenth Aureliano found a Jesus who still had a family. "Mom and Dad Stein," the second Jesus said when asked. "They don't call me son and I let them stay Jewish. They come twice a week."

On their next visit, the second Jesus asked his mother to get the book. Rachel Stein agreed without a demonstration of its importance because, as she admitted to her husband on the way to the car, she was "sick to death of miracles."

When the book came, armed with a record of his past that could not be erased by medication, the weeks passed more slowly but less disturbingly for the seventeenth Aureliano. "I was beginning to feel crazy," he would say to any Jesus who would listen. He started at the beginning of the novel since he had no way of knowing what he had forgotten. Eventually, at the bidding of three of the Jesuses who had taken a liking to him, he read aloud. Many times before, one Jesus or another had performed scenes from their translation of the Bible, but the stories were too familiar. The readings never went on for long. This time, every Jesus was held rapt to the point that when the book was destroyed the ward fell into a nearly irrevocable sadness.

It happened when, upon reading page 74, the seventeenth Aureliano was reminded that his language was Spanish. Immediately the book, an English translation, was indecipherable. In his anger he began barking at the fourth Jesus. "What good are words that mean nothing," he said. "Burn the whole damn lot of them."

The ninth Jesus, who knew the language but could not remember why, explained the message to the fourth. She was known to play jokes on people as they slept by performing a miracle to strike their beds aflame without a match. Before anyone could stop her, she had coerced the volume into a spitting fire that held everyone's attention until it was reduced to ash the color of the

cross on the seventeenth Aureliano's forehead. In the days following the bullet that pierced that cross, when the ward was once
again made up only of Christs, no Jesus would speak to the one
responsible for burning the book.

————

It was during the time when the Seventeenth Aureliano was waiting for his memory to arrive that the ninth Jesus displayed the
organizational prowess that would later make him important. A
fragile man who pronounced his new name with an accent, he
was one of the four incarnations that had no recollection of the
name he had used before divinity. All that remained of his memory
were childhood games of canasta that he often played again in
his head when he was alone. He meant to use the games as a
collection of facts to triangulate his origins and explain the *J*s he
said as *H*s, but the only thing that held any interest for him was
an aunt named Amaranta who always took a chair next to him at
the card table. He became most pleased when she dealt, as he
could still smell the lotion on her arms and feel the lax nylon of
her skin as she brushed against him. Though he couldn't know if
anything more had happened between them, he, even when re-
playing it from the hospital, would always pretend that he was
too young to know how to shuffle in the hopes that she might
take every hand.

If he had the rest of his memories to analyze, he might have
decided that it was those early games of canasta that had led to
the cockfights he organized as a hobby that became his vocation
before he was a deity. Even without knowing his own history, he
was often referred to as the "Jesus who makes things happen." It
was he who organized the football pool. Inevitably, the first Jesus
to fill in a square would be right so that the real contest was in

winning the raffle to choose first, of which they already knew the results. Nonetheless, they were interested in all of his games and when — while the seventeenth Aureliano waited for his book — he began a complicated system of betting on the war that played on their black and white television, the excitement was incendiary.

For capital, the ninth Jesus got the seventh Jesus to perform a miracle to transmute ordinary paper into communion wafers which she would allow to be used as poker chips only after she had de-blessed them. The ninth Jesus kept separate prizes for bombs dropped, targets named, targets hit, and total casualties, but the biggest jackpot was saved for the Jesus that could come closest to predicting the Secretary General's press release each evening. It was this category that was the most fun as it was the only one that was still in question because, as the sixth Jesus explained, "You can never be sure once they start talking." The betting went on for several nights before the seventeenth Aureliano spoke up against it.

"You," he exclaimed, "are no better than a pack of dogs. These people getting damned and here you are."

"You try to save them," the sixth Jesus said.

The seventeenth son of the Colonel thought about it and decided to wager seven wafers that the oil refinery would be the next to go. He began to play along with them and, in exchange for his newfound exuberance, they gave him extra stacks of Host because he squandered them so quickly.

The war had ended by the time the English translation of the book had been burned, and it was the ninth Jesus who provided some relief by translating the seventeenth Aureliano's request for a Spanish copy to the Steins. Once more, they agreed, and before long the seventeenth son of the Colonel was reading again. As they had done before, the circle of Jesuses gathered to listen. This

time, he was not alone in the center because they needed someone to translate. The ninth Jesus, as it turned out, did not speak
exceptional Spanish and there were many times that he remained
silent for entire passages before he was able to pick up the story
again. It was in this way that no Jesus ever learned that the Buendia
patriarch, the seventeenth Aureliano's grandfather, had eventually succumbed to the elements. In their imaginings he remained
eternally tied to the tree that, because the ninth Jesus misappre-
hended the word, was taken for a mailbox.

The seventeenth son of the Colonel became better humored
as the chapters were emptied of their secrets. "I am neither happy,"
he said, "nor worthless." He had tried to find a different word but
none had come, and ultimately it didn't matter because the ninth
Jesus was relieving himself in the toilet down the hall and no one
understood anything. Often, in moments without his interpreter,
he took great pleasure in stringing together proud sentences and
studying the Jesuses as they hung on every rotten syllable. But,
out of decency, he would not read aloud without the ninth Jesus.

One particularly humid afternoon, after the orderlies had
beaten the fourth Jesus for burning a week's worth of toiletries,
the seventeenth Aureliano, while reading, was reminded of his
half-brother that had led the fight against the banana company
in Macondo. "Jesus Christ," he said. "We can go on strike." He
waited for translation. All of them — even the fourth Jesus from
where her head lay split on her pillow — looked confused. "I
know how to do it," he said. Eventually, though none of them
knew their exact demands, they had fashioned picket signs out of
cloth and the sparkling grape juice they were allowed to use for
communion.

They started their strike by refusing medication. This wasn't
particularly effective since the orderlies had the license to beat
them until it was swallowed and, without it, miracles came so

easily that no Jesus retained a specialty. The seventeenth Aureliano
called that tactic off and unveiled a more direct plan. With thirteen Fathers on their side, the hospital staff was no trouble to
overpower directly. Soon he and the thirteen Jesuses had the run
of the place. None of them really wanted to go anywhere, so they
simply began to play foosball whatever the hour and watch the
television with the volume as loud as it would go. The seventeenth Aureliano tried to formulate another plan but, because he
had never resembled the other Aurelianos in his family, he was
uncomfortable with responsibility. "I am not meant to lead," he
said, and, with that, they began reading again.

As soon as, thanks to the book, the seventeenth Aureliano remembered the massacre that had killed his half-brother and most
of the population of Macondo, he called off the strike, demanded
that the orderlies be untied from the urinals where they had been
kept. The hospital returned to normal.

By this time, it had been several pages since he had re-read the
passage in which he had disappeared. He had become rather proud
of his exploits. In truth, he was thankful that he had gotten out
when he had. "This town has gone to shit," he said to the ninth
Jesus. Nonetheless, he was still interested and often smuggled
the book to the bathroom to read by himself. It was while sitting
on the toilet that he read page three hundred eighty and, without
warning, found himself back in Macondo. Two policemen who
had been chasing Aureliano for years, who had tracked him like
bloodhounds across half the world, came out from among the
almond trees on the opposite sidewalk and took two shots with
their Mausers which neatly penetrated his ashen cross.

His body fell to the bathroom floor where it was picked clean
by vultures.

———

In the days that followed, there were many theories about the Seventeenth Aureliano's death. The sixth Jesus was certain one of the orderlies had been responsible but, without proof, he could make no accusations and decided to return to the book for explanation. He tried to but could not speak the language and, anyway, questions about the possibility of the seventeenth Aureliano's resurrection were so loud he couldn't concentrate.

Finally, the sixth Jesus was able to convince the others that without the book they would never know how death worked for an Aureliano. "It is possible he has turned into a magpie or lives again as a macaw," he said. He was prepared to list other possibilities but did not have to. The room was filled with an eager rush of whispers and, after the sixth Jesus spoke again, they were quiet enough for the ninth Jesus to resume his reading.

Because he had never actually held it himself, the ninth Jesus could not remember where to start from and decided to begin at the beginning. The other Christs were strangely comforted by the experience and found new postures for their bodies so that they could concentrate as he read for several days without stopping. He began to wonder if it was a miracle that was keeping his mouth from getting dry; he was convinced he could finish the entire book without water. He wasn't able to, however, because before long the ward was interrupted by a new commotion.

"I have seen him," said the eighth Jesus. "In the hallway. I dipped a thumb in the bullet hole." The book was forgotten for the moment and all of them, much to the discomfort of the orderlies, hurried to the place where the son of the Colonel had appeared. In place of the seventeenth Aureliano was the lizard that had eaten from the floor of two grandmothers.

Upon seeing the lizard, the ninth Jesus remembered that his name was Omar Fuente and was heard to say, "Enough of your Aureliano." He remembered his business in cockfighting and decided he had done enough penance to return to the world with a single Hail Mary. He was granted permission to leave and received his belongings. Because the shirt they had held for him for seventeen years bore the image of a reptile, he opted to wear his hospital gown and would wear it until he returned to the ward, some years later, poisoned with enough headache medicine to block out the voice of the seventeenth son of the Colonel that grew louder when he slept.

Following the release of the ninth Jesus, the others grew despondent. One of them might have remembered that the book existed in English but, before they could, an insomnia plague fell upon the ward. They were unable to sleep and, without fatigue, could barely know anything. By this time, there were twelve of them and they all walked about, regardless of the time, in a curious fiction. "This has happened before," one of them said.

No one could remember what was being debated, but they argued for as long as they could remember how to. Without the past, they became stripped of the knowledge of miracles or of the will to perform them. Only the story of the seventeenth Aureliano — even untranslated — held their interest. Without sleep, granted an endless supply of time, the many Christs handed the book back and forth and attempted to understand.

✎ *The Dead* ✎

After Gretta told him of Michael Furey, Gabriel Conroy stayed awake for several hours, night-listening to a world suddenly too fragile for sleep. He sat on the edge of the bed where Gretta slept. Something in her chest rattled, just below her breathing. Every few minutes, Gabriel checked the weather. All night it was snowing. All night, he checked. He touched the thick window, pressing his palm to melt the frost. When the wind blew, the glass rattled. When the wind blew, he could hear the snow outside, faintly, like hundreds of brushes.

Many times, Gabriel returned to the bed. He sat, always in the same spot, one hand on Gretta's forehead. He closed his eyes and opened them. Twice he fished his watch from his vest and put it back, careful not to tangle the chain.

He did not lie down. He could not stop thinking. It was not his fault; he was not responsible for the epiphany that followed his wife's story. After all, he had not chosen to see things clearly.

Perhaps, if one were accustomed to epiphanies, one could sleep afterwards. This was Gabriel's second. The first had happened years earlier, as a child, and offered little in the way of guidance. It had been a dead chipmunk. He found it by himself on his aunts' property. It had been killed roughly, on purpose, by something with teeth.

Matted fur.

Blood.

A missing foot.

Gabriel had been fascinated.

He found a stick and poked the body, lifting and pushing it for several minutes, held rapt until he saw the maggots. One at first, then another, then a third. All moving. All not dead.

It was then that Gabriel *understood.*

—————— *An epiphany about the dead starts with the living.*

Before Gretta could tell him of Michael Furey, they had to attend a party, the same party as every Christmas. Though Gretta never spoke of it, Gabriel suspected that his aunts, Kate and Julia Morkan, intimidated her. He understood. His aunts were old but more vital — aggressively so — than they ought to have been. They made shows of their liveliness, eating and laughing with their mouths open, heads thrown back.

Gabriel imagined that they might have been pleasant to be around if they weren't so awfully attentive. They noticed everything. And, because of age, they were entitled to speak up. In their company, most people became shy, covering their mouths or averting their eyes. Once, several Christmases earlier, Greta had actually fainted.

Now, it seemed to Gabriel that Gretta could remain calm in their presence if she carefully prepared her appearance. She watched herself in mirrors, using her own image to steady herself. He asked her about it, once. She said he was imagining things.

—They're lovely women, she said.

Whatever her motives, as Greta prepared for the party where she would remember Michael Furey, she blinked and puckered patiently, getting her face just so. Because he understood her — few things are as important as understanding a wife of seventeen years, he thought — Gabriel did not mind waiting.

He stood at the window he would later stand at.

Everything was in place for the epiphany, but he wasn't ready.

—————— An epiphany arrives like a bee finds its way
through an open window.

While Gretta was getting ready, humming one of her made-up songs that she would deny having made up, Gabriel enjoyed the view from their hotel room, able to see most of Usher Island. It was snowing thick flakes, as plentiful as locusts. In the light from the street lamps — on already? were they that late? — it seemed as though the city was falling.

—————— An epiphany does not accompany every worthy moment.

Several hours later, after they returned from his aunts' party, Gretta told him of Michael Furey. They had been fond of each other once, she said, before Gretta and Gabriel had met. When she was young. They had taken grand walks. She described the landscape of Galway. She mentioned his hands. She mentioned his hair. He had a birthmark, moon shaped. His breath was often sour.

—Not unpleasant, Gretta said, but not fresh.

Gabriel had no idea that he was about to have an epiphany. Though his wife spoke more passionately than he was accustomed, Gabriel did not listen until she said that Michael Furey was dead. When he asked how he had died so young, she began to cry.

As he waited, he felt suddenly uneasy.

—He died for me, she finally said.

———— *An epiphany starts with the simple knowledge*
that everything is about to change.

Some time later, after Gretta had fallen into an unburdened sleep, Gabriel returned to the window where he had waited for her to get ready. It was still snowing, the flakes smaller and faster. He imagined Michael Furey, eyes as dark and steady as Gretta described. He imagined him outside, snow on his shoulders and collar, hair as wet as Gretta's last memory.

———— *An epiphany comes all at once.*

Standing at the window, watching the empty street, footprints covered, wife sleeping, Gabriel Conroy realized that all of the men who built the hotel were as dead as Michael Furey. His Aunt Julia would die soon. His wife was aging. Her face was not the same face that had tempted a young, sickly man to wait in the rain for a chance to see her.

———— *An epiphany requires messengers:*
swans or girls in white dresses.

On the way to their tardy arrival — after the Conroys got out of the cab and the driver had pulled the horses on — Gretta carried her shoes in a brown parcel. The ground was wet and she would not wear galoshes, no matter how many times Gabriel told her they were fashionable on the continent. It *was* snowing however, as soft and white as Gabriel had described from his hotel window, and she conceded that perhaps the galoshes would have made it easier to stay dry. Still, Gabriel knew she believed that grace of attitude counted for something, even as she gathered her skirt with one hand to keep it out of the slush.

He walked next to her, the excitement in his chest like a stubborn cough. He had his arm out for Gretta, but was occupied with the speech he would give after dinner, working and reworking the lines of Robert Browning he planned to use.

He was actually thinking of impending epiphanies. He did not expect to be the recipient but the instrument. He let himself imagine Browne and Freddy Malins coming away from the Browning — and his reading of it — positively bursting with insight. Though he'd had only one Gabriel was sure that others had epiphanies all the time, and that, maybe, he could help.

In his pocket, next to the Browning, he had a letter from his wife. It was a love letter, though it wasn't really *from* Gretta. He had written it himself, to her, before they were married, before the children, before the Christmas dances at his aunts' house. Sometime in the midst of their marriage, he found it. He kept it to remind him of who he had been. In the beginning. It was folded in thirds and then in half, kept safe in a dry pocket. Though he hadn't read it in years, he took the letter to the party. He took the letter everywhere.

> ——— *An epiphany never arises from an item*
> *or object one already cares about.*

In order to have his moment of insight, Gabriel Conroy had to embarrass himself with Lily, the caretaker's daughter. He had to listen to Browne ramble on about the great Campanini and Aramburo. He had to dance a series of awkward lancers with Miss Ivors. He had to change his speech to accommodate the evening. He had listen to Mr. Bartell D'Arcy sing *The Lass of Aughrim*. He had to watch Gretta listen to the song. He had to say goodnight to his aging aunts, and, after he and Gretta got out of their cab and made their way with D'Arcy to their hotel, he

had to want to catch up and whisper something foolish in his
wife's ear.

And after that, when they were finally alone with their bodies
and the early morning, Gretta had to tell him of Michael Furey
and the days in which she had first heard *The Lass of Aughrim.*

It was only then, while she slept — the whisper in her chest
hopefully just pleurisy — that he could listen to the snow falling
on the living and the dead.

————— *An epiphany requires orchestration.*

From their hotel to his aunts' house it was snowing. The flakes
were the size of thumbs, floating more than falling. Gabriel had
been to Usher Island at least once a year for as long as he wanted
to remember, and he had never seen snow so soft.

—It's usually more like rain, he said.

—I know, Gretta said, her arm loosely under his.

It was still sloppy, melting as it hit the street, and as soon as
the driver let them off, Gabriel was glad to have worn galoshes.
He liked the sound of the word, the funny influences and unlikely shape. Such words were what made English so sturdy, so
resourceful. He liked to say it aloud to Gretta.

—They're wearing galoshes all the time, he said. On the continent. It's galoshes everywhere.

She wasn't convinced. Still, he was surprised when, in the course
of greetings, she complained about his footwear.

—You wouldn't believe, she said as she changed into her shoes.
He wants me to wear them.

They were in the entryway; small piles of snow patterned the
floor. The cold hung in the air. She and Gabriel had to yell to the
aunts who lingered just out of the room, greeting their guests
without catching a chill.

Lilly, the caretaker's daughter, carried a small towel for spectacles. She was wet from carrying coats. A pile of belongings waited to be carried to the cloakroom. Her cheeks were flushed the way Gabriel remembered them. She was the reason the Miss Morkans' Annual Christmas Ball never fell flat. Every year, Gabriel looked forward to watching her whirl around the room with her silver tray of ales and hop bitters perched on a single hand.

He smiled at her. She looked at his feet.

Snow bunched on his galoshes like tiny toecaps.

—They wear them on the continent, he said, loudly enough for his aunts to hear.

—Always the continent, said Aunt Kate.

Gabriel didn't answer. He felt his cheeks go hot. It was no secret that he was sick of Ireland, but he had not anticipated it coming up so early in the night. And not by Aunt Kate. He suspected Miss Ivors was with them, and had spoken about his most recent article in the paper.

—Would've been here sooner, he said, but this one takes three mortal hours to dress herself.

He said it with just enough gaiety that everyone laughed, as he hoped they might. Gretta went upstairs, to the aunts. He took his and Gretta's things and followed Lilly to the cloakroom. She put a scarf on a tiny hook, and it fell off.

—Snow, she said.

—A night of it.

He looked at the ceiling and listened to the noises coming through, the pound and creek of feet, the muted strains of the piano. When he looked down, Lilly was folding his overcoat onto the highest shelf.

—Tell me Lilly, are you still in school?

—Oh, no sir.

—Oh, well, then, he said, his voice jolly and round. I suppose we'll be going to your wedding soon enough.

The girl turned to attend to his galoshes. She spoke over her shoulder, with an unselfconscious bitterness.

—The men now, they're all take and no give.

He colored again. He was tall and pale and knew he couldn't hide the smallest embarrassment. In his pocket, he felt a coin.

—Oh Lilly, he said, working the coin into her hands. It's Christmas.

—Oh, I don't, she said. Really I *couldn't*.

—Christmastime, he said, running up the stairs. Christmastime, he shouted from the top.

He had said the wrong thing, he was sure of it. He had made her feel small and poor and stupid. Gabriel's face was all sweat; his eyes stung. He fluttered his hands in a makeshift fan as it wouldn't do to arrive for the lancers already wet. He could hear the men dancing. The indelicate clacking of their heels reminded him that their grade of culture differed from his.

In the hall, he had a realization.

——— *An epiphany is not a realization.*

In the hall, listening, he realized that the verses he had chosen would elude his audience. He would alienate them. His entire speech was wrong. He would fail them the way he had failed Lilly. He would rework it. He began to revise, over the musings of the piano in the next room, over the graceless thunder.

He did not breathe confidently until it was over, until he danced the miserable lancers, until they ate and he spoke, and until he saw the dreadful Miss Ivors into a cab.

The hour was late, almost morning, when he finally dared to make himself tall again. He could see through the doorway, his

wife on the stairs, listening to Mr. Bartel D'Arcy. He could see
Gretta there, and feel his hands in his pockets. Gretta's hair had
been shinier other nights, younger nights. But watching her listen, her chin tipped slightly, her eyes closed just so, her hair had
never been so — he struggled to comprehend — so *fraught*.

———— *An epiphany about desire is not an epiphany.*

It felt like an epiphany.

As he watched her, he felt his wallet, where he kept the letter.
He watched her on the stairs, listening. He had a wonderful energy in his limbs. The remainder of the evening held no mystery.
He would touch her arm on the way home, through the cold and
slush. When they arrived, he would offer her warmth. He would
call to her. Watching her on the stairs, he knew he would call to
her. Gretta, he would say. She would come closer, and he would
tip her chin the way it tipped as D'Arcy sung to her.

———— *An epiphany does not affect any of the appetites;*
there are no signs.

Before he could relax into the evening there was a feast and his
speech to attend to. The table included a fat brown goose, a great
ham — stripped of its skin and peppered — and a round of spiced
beef. There were purple raisins and peeled almonds. They had a
dish of custard, an assortment of meat puddings, a rectangular
dish of smyrna dates, and a small bowl of chocolates. There were
pitchers of port and dark sherry. Lilly came around with her tray.

The staff was hurried but unemotional.

It was Gabriel that sliced the goose. After everyone had eaten
their fill, he began to speak.

—Ladies and Gentlemen. This is not the first time I have said these words under this roof, around this table. Most of us have been here before, the recipients — or should I say hostages — the hostages of this hospitality.

He paused, letting the joke play out.

—I am not known for my patriotism, but I mean this sincerely. No country, and I have been to more than a few, has our hospitality. Perhaps this is a curse, perhaps not. Either way, what the sisters Morkan preserve is a kindness unique in all the world.

He let them applaud briefly, before lowering his voice and affecting a stature of great seriousness.

—We are midstream of a new generation, a clever and industrious age.

He let them applaud again.

—But I must give pause. I must confess that for all this generation's savvy, its ideology and education, for all of this age's heaviness of intellect, we are on the verge of losing a different, more important kind of thoughtfulness, the kind exhibited by my aunts this evening. Let us hope that, even in the face of new ideas, let us hope that at gatherings such as this, we still speak of days past with pride and affection.

—Let us hope that we speak of those dead and gone great ones who the world will not willingly let die.

—We all have sadnesses. We could tell stories, every one of us.

———— *An epiphany often lingers in the periphery,*
like a waitress with a tray.

He could have listened to the snow then — it was falling — and watched his wife breathing. He could have — looking at Aunt Julia struggling to pay attention — considered their mortality.

Instead, he made his voice slightly brighter.

—Gatherings such as these can turn into such teary things. I will instead turn our attention to the living, to our hostesses. Julia and Kate.

He let the applause ring.

—And to my cousin, every bit as fair, Mary Jane. The three — what shall I call them — the three graces of Dublin.

Here they roared, as he hoped. He decided he could go ahead with his allusion. It was, after all, a common one.

—If I were Paris, I would hide under the table before choosing. I would hide.

—To them, he said, lifting his glass. To their humanity, their beauty.

As he hoped, Freddy Malins led the room in a few rounds of Jolly Good Fellow — Freddy Malins was always starting rounds of song so that no one would accuse him of being less fun than when he was drunk — and Gabriel Conroy sat down. No longer re-working the speech, his thoughts quieted, and he began to smile dumbly, a mere observer, as Lily brought out the cakes and preserves.

Again, he had a realization.

Lilly looked like Gretta when Gretta was younger.

She had been beautiful.

Watching Lilly, Gabriel *decided* to have the false epiphany he would have later. He would realize how beautiful Gretta still was. He didn't know when it would happen, but he knew that he would realize how much he still wanted her.

——— *An epiphany is not a casserole*
one can prepare ahead of time.

Before dinner, Gabriel danced with Miss Ivors.

—I have a bone to pick, she said.

He could tell by the way she was looking at him that the bone

was politics. She had arranged the sheets so that he was sched-
uled to dance with her three times.

—Oh, Gabriel said.

—How do you write for them? For *The Daily Express*?

He wanted to tell her that literature was above politics, but he
did not.

—Unless, she said, you are a West Briton.

And they danced. They danced more precisely than the rest of
the room, more precisely than Gretta, paired off with Freddy
Malins. Gabriel led Miss Ivors easily. She seemed to respond to
his inclinations rather than expectations. They altered steps here
and there without speaking.

—Gretta says she would love a trip, Miss Ivors said between
songs. She says she would like to go to Galway.

—Perhaps, Gabriel said. But I have a trip planned, the one I
take every year.

—Where?

—A trip.

—To the continent?

—Yes. A cycling tour. With some fellows. To the continent.
Miss Ivors looked at him.

—Galway would be good for Gretta.

—The continent helps me keep my languages.

—Galway speaks your language.

———— *An epiphany improves one's memory.*

By the time he helped serve the goose, Gabriel only thinly remembered talking to Miss Ivors. It wasn't until later, when Gretta
told him about Michael Furey, that the conversation returned.

—So this is what that Galway nonsense is about.

—I don't understand, Gretta said.

—You wish to see him.

He didn't stand up as he waited for her response. He pulled at an ear and felt his color return more fully, more hotly than at the party.

—He's dead. Many years dead.

As she cried — the coals of his anger doused —he felt like vapor, like steam. He felt the epiphany, the first of it at any rate. He felt it in his vanished plans.

He had wanted to call to her. He had planned on saying her name, saying it softly while she undressed, unaware of his desire. He had wanted to be rough and sincere, smooth but hard, whatever she would have of him. He had wanted to tower over her, to shrink beneath her touch, to fit himself around and above and below her. He had reread his letter. He had recalled moments of their secret life, mundane snippets and a generically specific day, their hands together while they watched a glassmaker heat and melt and blow.

He had wanted her.

He had let himself want her.

———— *An epiphany arrives like heartburn.*

—So you were in love, he said, though he knew he meant something else.

—I was well enough with him then.

—How did he die at so young an age? Consumption?

—I think he died for me.

———— *An epiphany leaves one utterly inept.*

He knew he should do something but didn't speak for some time. He bowed his head and offered his hand to her. Hers was moist and warm; it did not respond to his touch but he continued to caress it, the way he had his letter.

—It was in the winter when I was going to leave my grandmother's and come up here to school. He was ill at the time and would not be let out of his lodgings. He was in decline, they said.

Gabriel nodded but she wasn't watching him.

—He was very fond of me. So gentle. And a beautiful voice.

Again he nodded. He stroked her hand.

—The night before I left, I heard stones, small stones, against my window. I couldn't see, the window was so wet. I went outside, and there he was in the garden, at the end of the garden, shivering.

—Did you send him away?

—I told him the rain would be his death. He said he did not want to live. He was standing there, dripping and cold, at the end of the wall, under a tree.

—Did he go home?

—Yes. And a week later he died.

She began to sob again.

Gabriel continued to hold her hand until he felt as if he were intruding on her grief. He let her hand fall gently and withdrew to the window.

———— *An epiphany is not the same thing as bad news.*

That was that.

———— *An epiphany may or may not be borne out in action, but an epiphany does not find its currency in words..*

He did not lie down. He went to the window and returned to the bed. He put his hand against the thick glass. He retrieved his watch from his vest and put it back, carefully. He listened to the snow.

He heard Gretta's labored breath.

He heard the hotel creak and rattle.

He heard someone in a nearby room, unable to sleep.

❧ How Bartleby Spent the Night in the Detroit House of Corrections Preferring Not to Contemplate the World, Preferring Not to Start His Life Over Again ❧

(Exhumed, Impossible Notes for a Vague Report; Some Blood Squeezed from Canonical Stones; New Shoes for an Old Horse Called *The Meaning of Life*; A Happy Ending; A Reverie for Dead-Wall Reveries)

THE BASIC STORY:

1. A nineteenth century man discovers a sad truth — that there is no such thing as an original, meaningful life story — and, out of grief, refuses several opportunities to reclaim his humanity before withdrawing from the world, being jailed, and dying in an obscure, self-fulfilling prophecy.

A SECONDARY STORY:

1. A twentieth century girl plans an essay about how, after being jailed for shoplifting, she reclaimed her humanity when she returned to the suburbs and felt plush carpeting beneath her feet.

TERTIARY STORIES:

1. A narrator (myself) steals the nineteenth century's story.

2. A narrator (myself) steals the twentieth century's method of presentation.

ABOUT THE CELL BARTLEBY SHARED WITH THE GIRL:

1. It is a chronological impossibility, but all fictional jail cells are impossibilities. Gravity holds, in fictional jail cells, only because we decide to allow it. It is possible that Bartleby has been in every fictional jail cell since the beginning of time and that narrators have simply chosen not to mention his presence.

2. When the narrator (myself) steals fictional events — even famous ones — and alters them, only fictional history is altered. This is less dangerous than in time travel movies where one can accidentally prevent one's father from meeting one's mother.

    One might say that all stories are fictional jail cells, artifices that hold characters who change or do not change. All descriptions of fictional jail cells sound familiar, built of human experience and sound, character and phoneme, unspoken desire and the glottal stop.

CHARACTERS:

1. The narrator myself. The author/lawyer figure. If I were a nineteenth-century narrator, you would recognize my coat and tie,

my facial hair, and my cravat or whatever. Only a mole — a mark that reminds you of something geographical, a Canadian Province — would distinguish me from a gentleman or lady who came to your drawing room a fortnight ago with a story that stuck in your chest like a dram of white vinegar.

Reasons To Tell This Too-Familiar Tale

1. Because they have been dispossessed of their narratives, these scriveners, these writers who have never scriven their own words, choosing instead to copy yours, mine.

2. Because Bartleby, this specific scrivener I will speak of, has wormed his way into my day-to-day like a new invention, a shiny faucet, toaster, or heated towel rack that I can not imagine the world without.

3. Because of the girl. Written more than a hundred years after Bartleby's, her story has never been part of this story. She is not a scrivener but a student, learning new rules. In a few years, she will be cautious of the first person in a formal essay, careful not to end a sentence with a preposition.

Characters:

1. Bartleby, the scrivener. With his curt and allegorical politeness — his mouth wore but a single shape, a half-pursed smile beyond meaning — Bartleby is the mute first-person narrator, a sealed envelope from heaven, the real story masked by a forest of well-intended retellings, a veritable tome of unreadable

exposition. He was a smokejumper with a wife and kids; he kept his money in a burlap sack beneath the floorboards of the guest bedroom where his youngest baby slept. Or he was a mime; face white as an inverse photo of the blankest slate, he made the glass box collapse, summoned the wind and then kept it from stealing his hat. Or he lived for two and half years under the Metro in Paris, playing a flute for change, using crumbs of cheese to catch his dinner, mostly rats.

I could have loved him.

2. The girl. Bartleby's opposite. Where he is mute, she is falsely forthright. She is the first-person narrator who changes her history. She has a fake ID in her stolen purse. It has your picture on it. Your address.

EVENTS:

1. In need of another scrivener, I hired Bartleby for a good wage. I found him a most peculiar man; I was drawn to him. I teased him about his silence, waggled my finger and asked him questions so he would surprise us with his speaking. But I found myself thinking, while documents waited for my attention, that his voice was like fine china, seldom used, composed of something as anachronistic and essential as bone.

2. Bartleby did not work. He stared out his window, which was my window.

3. I eventually moved Bartleby to an obscure room with no way out.
   I hope he knew his view from memory.
   I hope those days in prison, without his window, were not

terrible ones.

I hope that, even in that prison, he could discern new patterns in his old wall: three gray bricks, four red, three gray. I hope he could imagine himself microscopic, inching along a highway of mortar, endlessly strolling around and among and in-between ranks and ranks of similar bricks. I don't know if this is what he liked to do from my window. Perhaps he just looked. Perhaps, when confronted with the unrelentingly empty wall, he imagined himself a brick: useful if not unique, rough to the touch, and completely nerveless.

4. Bartleby expired. It was hard to tell when it happened. He seemed to be dying forever and not at all, the way he lived, slowly and self-censored. The evidence of his passing was no different than the evidence of his other, less distinguished days and nights.

CHARACTERS:

1. The author/lawyer figure. I pull strings. Typically, it is up to me to weave a story's elements into a thematic thread, raising an unexpected, plywood sun in the middle of the reader's living room.

2. Bartleby. He had distinguishing marks, like anyone. A port wine stain across both butt cheeks, a chipped incisor, maybe even a stainless-steel piercing on the flap of skin between his thumb and forefinger. He had birth records, complete with half-moon footprints and a mother's maiden name.

The only specifics I knew of him were his sturdy-blue Everyman clothes.

3. Turkey. A scrivener who worked for me. A good man in the mornings, a handful after his noontime drink.

4. Nippers. A scrivener who worked for me. A handful in the mornings, a good man after his noontime drink.

5. The girl. She stole gloves from Branden's, that excellent store, and fought with a sometimes boyfriend named Simon. She was near tears and crazy in the holding cell, sharing the room with Bartleby.

   She is our modern loophole, the newly forged second tine of his forked path. What drove him to his dead wall will save her.

Events:

1. Instead of improving, Bartleby became obstinate. Among scriveners, there is a custom of giving the final work a collective read-through to ensure perfect copy. When it was Bartleby's turn to read, he said simply, "I would prefer not to."

   The first time he said it, I was enamored by the phrase. I put up a show of consternation but, for the rest of the day, I said it to myself, waiting for the crosswalk, watching Jeopardy, making dinner in my single kitchen.

   I imagined him saying it, the shape of his mouth.

2. Uncomfortable with my interest, I offered to pay him to disappear.

3. He did not leave. Soon he preferred not to do any work at all. I moved his desk to a back room to avoid explanations. It was as if he had been waiting for me to move him all along, as if he

had applied for the job in the hopes that he would end up there, by himself, in the hottest room of the building.

4. He began to live in his office, which was my office. He slept in an undershirt and, during work hours, stood in front of his window with his brick wall.

5. I've always enjoyed going to the office on Sundays. The streets empty for church; the city smells better when people are praying.

I must confess that my reasons for working on Sundays were slightly different in the period following Bartleby's arrival. I did not like thinking about him in my home.

Several of those empty Sundays, when I tried to use my key to open my office door, Bartleby told me to wait while he gathered his things and changed out of his nightshirt. He suggested that I walk around the block a few times.

Had he spoken more, he could have talked me into anything.

6. Bartleby's presence began to affect my business. My author/ lawyer friends wanted to know about his back-story: did he have family in the metro area? was he a trauma survivor? They spent whole afternoons wondering about Bartleby, inventing explanations.

Part of me wanted Bartleby gone because, with all of the speculation, he made us unproductive. But there was something else. I didn't like the way he made me feel. The more questions my friends asked — the more possible Bartlebys they constructed — the more I became simultaneously desperate. Without knowing his story, I was unsure I knew anything, and yet, knowing him would have cheapened a good mystery.

And there was something else still.

I just wanted to know him.

7. When Bartleby would not leave, I moved out from under him. He found my office to be his alone; Nippers, Turkey, and I had simply vanished.

8. I heard that he would be forcibly removed from the abandoned building so I attempted to intervene; I did not want him jailed or hurt; I merely didn't want him in my building, occupying the same story.

I made one last attempt to talk to him. He was in a deep and lonesome reverie, his face against the glass of his dead window. We had a routine mastered by then, and as I told him what would happen if he did not move, our roles were the same. I was close to shaking, and, whatever I asked, he preferred not to.

9. I did not visit immediately. When I finally arrived with food and money, he was a gaunter, more skeletal version of his gaunt and skeletal self. Looking at him then, thinly preserved, I barely saw him. There was something incorporeal, like the living Bartleby had passed through an hour earlier. Never substantial, it was as if he had become his own footprint or contrail, evidence that would have already dissipated if there had been a window with a breeze.

10. While Bartleby expired in his hard-to-realize way, the girl was home again, washing her hands, amazed by the sensation of the water, waving her fingers back and forth through the steady stream.

FOOTNOTES TO THE EVENTS

1. All I have learned of Bartleby, in the years following his death,

is a rumor: before I hired him, he may have worked in a dead-letter office.

Oh Bartleby! To continually handle these dead letters — does it not sound like dead men — sorting them for the fire! To be employed in not one but two professions author/lawyer figures can use as metaphors for hopelessness!

2. *Dead Letter Office* is an R.E.M. album. Bartleby must have heard it a dozen times working for me. He never said anything.

The songs are mostly covers.

What Lit Crit. Has Said Of Bartleby:

1. The repetition of Bartleby's "preferring not to" becomes an ironic mimesis by which the reader comes to understand Bartleby's true desire: to fade into the background, thereby beating inevitability to the punch.

2. The epistemology of Bartleby's conclusion is less important than its phenomenology.... We are made to clearly observe the symptoms of his metaphysical condition because he would "prefer not to" register his complaint directly.

3. The ineffable epiphany that Bartleby has enjoyed, prior to [this story's] beginning, is simply the realization that no experience is truly unique.

4. Bartleby has been correctly described by [other literary critics] as allegorical. However, it is not Bartleby who serves to metaphorize the reader. Bartleby is [this story's] hero because

his unremarkable story *avoids* being an unremarkable story. Because as [this story] lumps all stories into the category of The Same Old Story, Bartleby is the only character that the reader is *not* allowed to read as a stand-in for him/herself. Bartleby's lack of action becomes redemptive. Every other character, [myself] included, becomes a collective, allegorical character with a universal referent.

5. [W]ithout meaning to, Bartleby offers a path to liberation....[F]or this Bodhisattva, enlightenment is a passive resistance to experience, a refusal to accrue the usual phenomenological stickers on one's existential luggage.

6. A strange wrinkle to [fifth critic's] depiction of Bartleby as a Bodhisattva figure is that the theory, by implication, renders Bartleby's path as derivative of another: the Buddha's.... [E]ven enlightenment is not a unique condition.

7. While [fifth and sixth critics] search the past for iconography that might resonate with Bartleby, his circumstance also has its modern equivalent. The "proofing" sessions in which Bartleby would "prefer not to" participate have an eerie resemblance to today's writers' workshops.

WHAT LIT CRIT. HAS SAID OF THE GIRL:

1. When, glad to be home, she washes her hands after spending the night in jail, she accepts the details of the essay we never read, the car in the driveway, the way she fits into the clothes worn by the medicated women she thought she abhorred.

2. She does not need to complete the essay.

3. The strange and resonant beauty of [another author/lawyer figure] giving us nothing more than the girl's notes is this: form is at odds with content. While [the girl] chooses to live an anonymous life, she [the other author/lawyer figure] finds a wholly original way to tell the story.

IRONY CONCERNING THE FIRST APPEARANCES OF THE CHARACTERS

1. Bartleby appeared in the world-before-Derrida. His dead-wall reveries took place when a cigar was just a cigar, when face-value couldn't be deconstructed, when an author/lawyer figure could still reserve a seat at the canonical table.

2. Even as I tell his impossible-to-tell story, Bartleby is part of the canon — his assertion that all stories are unoriginal serves as a clause that limits the size of canonical family gatherings. Because he said it (or implied it) first, all future author/lawyer figures who encounter similar characters must sit at the kids' table.

3. The girl — with her unorthodox story — has been elected the canon's homecoming queen.

WHAT I HAVE LEARNED SINCE I FIRST TOLD YOU OF BARTLEBY

1. His epiphany was a little one. Who cares. I shouldn't have abandoned him. I miss him and that dopey look on his face.

What I Can Do About It

1. Because he is fictional and I am fictional, I can block his dead window, forcing him to look at me. You have to believe me when I tell you, right now, that he gives in and looks me up and down.

   After small talk that he prefers not to make, he prefers not to beat me in chess. Later, he prefers not to sketch me in pencil but relents after I draw him with funny teeth. Finally, I make him walk with me to the closest bar. We feed quarters into pinball machines and jukeboxes and listen to the same songs a thousand others have requested. Soon, the hour is late enough that he can no longer know for sure whether or not he prefers to follow me home.

❧ Real-Time Video of Dead People You Want to Have Coffee With ☙

PROLOGUES AND STARS

Watching this, you have as good a seat as anyone. Technically, I am closer — just a wall away from what we've started calling the ghost of William Stafford — but, as distance goes, geography is overrated.

What I can see, you can see.

Every time the outside camera switches on, we — the three of us in the house and you at home — see the same thing. We see meteors. A dozen at a time. They flutter and spiral, less like rocks than burning insects, a series of short-lived stars that descend into the hills behind the house.

Something this beautiful should be seen first hand. It should be fully experienced. We should be fending off bugs, smelling cow shit, straining our necks — this should not come without a cost.

But, tonight, we see the meteors on a computer screen.

Light has been amplified, converted into code, turned back into light.

Though we — Tito, Wellbutrin, and I — disagree on the specific reasons for being in William Stafford's Kansas estate, we agree about the basics. We buy houses that belonged to dead writers.

We set up cameras and broadcast Internet video.

The three of us are off-camera in a walk-in pantry. The space is small and hushed, surrounded by three tiers of shelves and a history of emptiness. There is barely enough room for us, our tech, and an emergency toilet.

Wellbutrin says it's been twenty years since Stafford lived here. He wrote in the study upstairs. He made love in the master bedroom. He kept canned peaches or tomatoes where we are hiding. He listened to the house at night, its structural complaints. He must have heard its other noises too, cocking his head in the pink light of a thunderstorm as the house resisted the wind.

When we bought it, we saw the property records. Twenty years ago, when Stafford moved to California, he sold the place to a family named Peterson. A few other families lived here while Stafford was enjoying his best years as a poet, but the place was empty by the time he died.

We do not use our real names. The others know I was born Theresa but do not mention it. They know that I was Theresa years ago, before my acting career, when my parents were still alive.

This is not our first famous house.

We have rules.

We stay off-camera so we won't alter your experience of the estate. Any description — a single-story three bedroom with good fixtures and bad plumbing — is interpretation, even if it's true. Though the specifics of our reasons for doing this differ, all three of us agree that we should let the houses speak for themselves. This means not changing anything, not redecorating, not even cleaning. Even if other people lived here in-between, the houses are fossils and we leave them be.

The pantry is tiny. In the light of the computer, the air is visible. Twenty years of dust moves every time we do. The smallest motion scatters millions of startled molecules.

Completely still for a fifth of a century, this claustrophobic world will not stop moving: Tito has a knee twitching, Wellbutrin chews his licorice, the dust swims like a tide.

It occurs to me that, contained in the tiny box of our monitor, the outside world is exempt from the science of cause and effect. I can see the falling stars, a hundred explosions a minute, but nothing changes in here. In here, the outside is just information.

Though nothing is going on inside the house to rival the meteor shower, the camera switches feeds to take a tour of Stafford's empty rooms. When the outside comes back on, Wellbutrin sighs his appreciation. Our monitor is the highest resolution Tito could get, but I still don't like it. The video is jerky. The meteors bob as they fall, like clothes pulled in on a windy line.

If I complain Tito will swear the tech is top shelf.

Best of the master's tools, he'll say.

I know that he has numbers and jargon, but I don't trust computers. I don't think they are malicious or anything. I just think they're holding something back, like a bad pinochle partner. I trust a monitor less than a painted window.

If there were any other way to do this, to you show you, I'd take it. As it is now, I chose to remain ignorant of our tech. My ignorance turns the box into magic.

I've never been attracted to philosophy, but, during our thirty-six hour broadcasts, abstraction is as natural as a travel game in a cross-country station wagon.

In this half-lit space, there are facts. I can touch my own face. Tito and Wellbutrin are bent together, hard at work. I am behind them, with a hand on Tito's back, occasionally leaning in to hear or see. When we speak it is in whispers, as if we were just a few feet off stage, as if there were actors to throw off, or a crowd to distract. As if we weren't a thousand miles away from you. As if you were watching.

Right now, everything — you, the meteorological ghost of Stafford, China, sunlight — everything outside this pantry exists in the same proximity to us, knowable only through the mediums of the computer and faith.

It has only been twelve hours.

"Come on," Tito says to the box, "go back outside." He is a small man, too small for his thinking. His body seems to flap in the steam of his ideas. He rocks in his chair, kicking his feet in a lopsided rhythm. He pulls at an ear with one hand while the other plays with the zipper of his red sweatshirt. The cameras switch back and forth automatically, randomly, but he obviously has his favorites. "Yeah, yeah, yeah, yeah," he says when the meteors come back on-screen. "Choke on the fatty cords of your forgetting."

He is speaking to America again. He is a Marxist, though he swears it's several prefixes more complicated than that. His part in our undertaking is strictly political. For him, the images — the empty house, Stafford's former property — all of it is a revolution of memory. He says that memory is a petri dish for love cells. He says that consumerism is the religion of amnesia. He says that by sending this footage into your home — even if you aren't watching — the three of us are the supernova remedy to the twenty-first century, a madcap antidote to a madcap poison.

Wellbutrin is taller than Tito, and heavier. For him, our purpose in these houses is educational. We are in the business of exhumation and reanimation, bringing an author's work to contemporary life by providing the context of his or her living.

When we finish the thirty-six hour broadcast — all of the houses get a day and a half — he will write an essay, posted on the website. He has explained to us, several times, what he will say about Stafford. He will talk about plain language, words as small and versatile as linguistic atoms or DNA, words as simple as rocks.

As soon as the meteors started, Wellbutrin gave another lecture, this time about a single poem. In the poem, a star hits California, in the hills behind Stafford's house. The rock is shown over television, and roped-off, available for viewing during business hours. When Stafford goes to investigate, he is told classified information by a security guard. He begins to wonder what it would take to be the guard, to have his job. The guard explains that, among other things, one must swear allegiance to the state of California. Stafford resists, holding out the possibility that, if a star were bigger than the state, he might swear allegiance to it instead.

Eventually, Stafford agrees to remain loyal to California.

In his lecture, Wellbutrin made it clear that Stafford was bullied. He said the poem was about the unknown, about the difference between you and me, about uncertain futures mitigated by the state.

Though I thought it was all a little too close, the last part caught Tito's attention and, together, he and Wellbutrin rallied around their respective, abstract ideas of our project, equal parts revolution and junior-high field trip.

In textbooks, history is a garage sale, a gaudy collection of half-broken toys and funny clothes that couldn't possibly fit anymore. We put it on acid free paper. We want it to be preserved, embalmed, restored.

We film costume dramas and dramatic reenactments. Every

year several thousand people dressed in historically accurate Civil War uniforms rush down hills and across fields in the same formations used by running men a hundred and fifty years ago.

With no one dying, the war is a lot of fun.

I think that what we're doing here is simple.

We're giving you a lengthy glimpse inside houses where the once-famous were once alive.

We're looking for ghosts.

Stare long enough and any place is haunted.

To be honest, I don't really care about the specifics of these houses. My interest in the past is about proof that it existed at all. I've never had memories of grandparents. I can't imagine my own parents as having been children. I never really saw them age. Part of me still has a hard time believing that Shakespeare wasn't my seventh grade English teacher making it up, writing the next scene while we were playing on the tornado slide. Even my own childhood seems like a fabrication.

None of this should matter, but I am afraid of death.

I remember how it started. There was a time when I wasn't scared, and then suddenly, irrevocably, I was. I was six when it happened. I was still Theresa. I didn't start acting for another year. My parents were alive for another four.

At school, I learned the sun would swallow the earth in several hundred thousand years — I don't remember how long — right before its own death. Even though I knew I would be gone long before the sun exploded, the image of it expanding, swallowing the earth in fire, and then receding into blackness, provided the cinematography for my first nightmares.

Soon after, I discovered the Big Bang. I was every bit as frightened by a sudden beginning as I was by a quicksand end. Instant history was as scary as the final, vanishing chapter.

I am here, in these houses, because I want proof of a back-story. I want prologues, not just for our subjects but for all of us. I want evidence that Tito has been a gazelle, a thousand butterflies. I want to know that Wellbutrin has taken handfuls of water from every river in Austria, dug for silver in mines that have been closed a hundred years. I want a trap door before conception, a three-act play on the other side of the opening stage directions.

I see meteors. I want to know where they came from, what they were before our atmosphere. Watching them, it occurs to me that they are the only new light in the sky. Even with different histories they fall the same way.

One after the next, they become stories about fire.

I don't know if it is psychosomatic, or if I'm allergic to the room, or if I just forgot how to breathe, but I am coughing. I try to steady, but I suck in more dust. I can see it puff in and out of my mouth and nose. I cough harder. I feel my lungs heaving, heavy with the gritty air. My hands push against Tito and Wellbutrin so that I won't lose my balance. I stagger and sway.

Eventually, when I don't stop, the others have to turn to me. For almost a minute they look startled and uncertain, unprepared for dealing with my physical body. Tito gets a bottle of water to my lips. I try to swallow, but my tongue is arid, and I am still hacking. Most of the drink spits into the air. Tito doesn't give up, trying in vain to keep it close to my mouth. He is persistent but easily spooked, like he's poking a stick at something poisonous.

When the coughing finally subsides, my shirt is completely wet. Without a change of clothes in the pantry, there is nothing to do but take the bottle of water between my hands and sit down. Tito and Wellbutrin immediately turn back to the box.

The camera switches.

I watch the old rock, the new, new light.

Ghostboy Dies in Tragic Mishap

Our thirty-six hours over, we are able to relax.

When we stopped at midnight, I went straight to bed. Alone with myself, I didn't sleep much. The bed provided a much more pleasant insomnia than I had enjoyed in the pantry.

The three of us are in the front yard now, enjoying the wind.

Until we can close a deal on new property, we will stay in the Stafford house.

While I chased myself around the wide savanna of my bed, Wellbutrin finished his write-up. He seems lighter for it, with more color in his face. He has his stunt kite out in the yard. The kite has two strings. Wellbutrin is steering, leading it toward the ground, pulling it back into the sky. His face is soft but thoughtful as he makes decisions based on string tension and reflex. He swings the kite in a broad circle.

"If only Yeats' falcon was this responsive," he says. "Widening gyre my ass."

Occasionally, against better judgment, he gives the reins to me.

If I'm not doing anything active, you could watch me for days and think my hands were whole. Flying the kite, it becomes obvious that I have no fingers. Though my thumbs are strong, and I'm concentrating, I soon lose one or both of the strings and we have to chase the kite as it bounces to the highway.

An hour or so later they will let me try again.

These afternoons after a broadcast are not about good choices. It is better to chase the kite. Even Tito — who normally claims that exercise is a capitalistic vulture feeding on our self-disgust — runs as fast as he can.

We break sweats and turn ankles on the loose gravel.

About three in the afternoon, I fall. Something in my elbow gives. The joint gets puffy and stiff. Twenty minutes later, the boys trip over each other and end up pulling rocks out of their bloody shins with tweezers. Soon we are running again.

Tonight we will need ice for the swelling. For now, we can't stop.

The burn in our calves is somehow more than information.

Even when we aren't broadcasting from the houses of dead people, Tito does his best to make the web site interesting. Every morning he takes his coffee by himself and has a few hours alone with the tech. By lunch, he lets Wellbutrin and I join him for a virtual demonstration of his improvements and modifications.

Today, the third after the Stafford transmission, Wellbutrin has prepared lamb kabobs, and Tito has a present for me. He has finally finished the Ghostboy archives. While we eat, he shows off how convenient the text is, how easy it is to see the new and tragic footage.

No one says anything — I can hear them chewing, waiting for my reaction. I haven't seen it since just after the accident happened. For that matter, I haven't seen a picture of Ghostboy in almost two years. Still, the face is just as I remember it, wide-eyed and androgynous, a younger version of my own.

And now, thanks to Tito, if you come to the website, you can see the famous final minutes, the explosion that history will tell you is the end of Ghostboy's life.

When we finish with the footage, Wellbutrin drapes a lazy leg over Tito's knee. This sort of thing has been happening more and more, usually for twenty minutes at a time. It is a strange symbiosis. Wellbutrin is gracious and easy but not trusting. And Tito is not a man of small interludes. But they sit like this, Wellbutrin's foot dangling against gravity, his body vulnerable and no longer solitary while Tito's knee must resist the shaking pace at which his body normally runs.

Tito cues up my accident again. He starts it from the top, lets his hand fall on Wellbutrin's arm. I know they are romantic, or at least pathologically close, but I will not ask for clarification.

I've always thought they were together, even before they started touching like this. There is ample grace and antagonism between them; both qualities spill out in unforced ways. With me, they never say much, never open wounds that they do not mean to. Even Tito has boundaries with me.

I watch them touching.

On the screen an incarnation of myself dies.

After lunch, we move to the sun porch.

Tito made lemonade and spiked it. He has a cigar because he's been meaning to smoke them forever. Wellbutrin doesn't want the smoke in his face, says it will make him want a cigarette, so I sit between them.

"Boyfriend," says Tito.

I am not sure if I feel up to it, after seeing the last footage of Ghostboy, but I nod.

"Have I told you about Victor?"

"No," they say.

I nod again.

They are both looking at me, from either side.

"I was fifteen. He was twenty-three, a sous chef on set for *Stranger Death*."

"Sous-per," says Tito.

"He used to slip notes in my meals. AM HOT, ARE YOU? SAUCE BOY SEEKS SAUCY GIRL. That sort of thing."

"And you fell in love and had kids."

"We slept together twice before he was fired."

They smile a little.

I never give them more than a few sentences. I like to watch Tito and Wellbutrin imagining the man, wondering if he had an earring, a little tummy, a pet snake.

Though Victor was very real — it was actually several months before he was let go — many of the boyfriends I give them are complete fictions.

The rest of the afternoon, while the others dodder about the place, I can't stop watching my supposed death. When I asked him to, Tito fixed it to play again and again without being asked, a mantra that moves in all directions from our Kansas.

The actor is young, a horror genre unto himself. He is known only as Ghostboy, pale and bony in the cheeks. Androgynous as ever, he is always referred to as being male because no one is sure and he lived in America.

He wears dark fabric that sways loose, away from the chest. The clip is from *The Fear Helix*. He holds his body with the same limp anxiety that he used for *Stranger Death* and the serial work he did for television in *Hallowed Hours*, but there is something else, a decadent lilt in his movement, a rigor to his eyes that brings a resonance he never hit in his early work. Always a conduit for death, even in the first thing he did, there is an extra gravity this time, in this scene. This time, somewhere in the loose glow of his cheeks, there is comprehension. He is finally more than scary.

He is on a ladder, in a murky library. There is a book with cheesy ornamentation perched on a far shelf and open and spine down. The pages flutter as he climbs.

By itself, on the web site, the clip has no back-story. In the movie, the book was a primer for the barrier between life and afterlife. Ghostboy was fetching it for reasons of universal import.

According to the AP article Tito has attached, the book was meant to explode. It was to flash and smoke, to pull away from Ghostboy, to curl up in ash. There were to be chemicals and color, science and mirrors. It was to look brighter and hotter than it was. It was this stunt that killed him. You can see it start by his fingers, orange against the blue of the room. It crawls. In his eyes there is something, still not fear.

Tito included audio. The lines are not from the scene, but the words are unimportant. The voice itself is all that matters, Ghostboy at his most famous. His voice is multivalent, a thousand octaves, nasal and throat. Even uploaded and transmitted, it rumbles and purrs, catches somewhere in your head, the resonant frequency of dying birds.

I can't do anything about it.

If I speak above a whisper, I am terrifying.

Tito once compared my voice to recordings of Plath. Wellbutrin disagreed. He said that Plath sounded alive in spite of herself. He said that I sound the other way around, like I am trying to talk myself back to life.

We are not old, the three of us. Tito is the youngest. Twenty-three last November. Wellbutrin was thirty a few weeks ago, the end of June. I am twenty-seven. March second.

I'm attracted to birthdays for the same reasons that I am interested in history. I am comforted by growth rings.

At dinner, though I know it will do no good, I ask Wellbutrin about his name again. I know that Tito's was Jeremy Watkins. They both know that mine was Theresa Muncie. Only Wellbutrin won't tell. Only Wellbutrin admits he has anything to hide.

"You know I can't tell you who I was," he says. "He'd find me."

"It's simple really," Tito says. He touches Wellbutrin's hand as he talks. "Wellbutrin is claustrophobic with Plato. Afraid of an archetype, the first self, the first him, pole-catting around, different than him prime."

Wellbutrin looks stricken enough that I can't tell if he agrees with Tito's explanation. I watch him until we are finished and begin to clean up. I think Tito is wrong, that Wellbutrin just doesn't want to go back to being who he was.

I think about my own name.

We wash dishes, mainly bowls.

There are soup bits and melted ice cream in the dishwater.

"I was named for my mom," I say. "So that I'd be like her."

"Did it work?" Wellbutrin asks. He looks like he'd believe it either way.

"My parents are dead," I say.

"That's the spirit," Tito says.

But Wellbutrin looks uneasy. He moves, as he always does, with more control than either Tito or myself. Though I feel close to both of them, there is a simpler complexity to him, a symmetry to his lack of balance that is easy to relax into. I want to agree with him and usually do.

Even as we remain silent while we rub our dishes dry, I know he is right, that I was my parents' daughter, and that I started out usual, tickled flowers the same as anyone. I know that, like him — probably Tito too, though he'd never admit it — who I was would not want anything to do with who I've become.

My first role came at five. There was an ad for extras on the radio and I talked my parents into it. They were kindly, drove me to the audition. We were all taken on. My name, my real name, was to appear on the credits. I was cast in a horror mini-series, as part of a mob of dead children.

It wasn't like I was a morbid kid. I knew I wanted to act, but I thought it would be something like *Annie*, something with singing. As it turned out, I was good at dead. Better than the rest. By then I was scared and the makeup and posture was only a tap into my fascination with other, smaller kinds of death. I was able to remember a rotting squirrel brought down by my parent's dog. I focused on the buzz of flies, the skitter of maggots.

And my voice was already something. The only one of the children that had a speaking part was obviously less eerie than I was. He was fired a few days into the shoot. They didn't want to bother the writer, who was on to something else, so they didn't change the gender.

It turned out I was scarier as a boy. They listed me as Ghostboy and formed a dizzy legal team to bury the trail, make sure that I never came out as Theresa.

The mini-series did well and I had top billing on the posters when it went to rental. Offers came in for Ghostboy, and my parents found a way to move to California. When they died, I kept working.

My career lasted almost ten years — three different action figures — and no one knew my name. I didn't have to act like a boy because no one knew I wasn't one. I made good money. I did three seasons of television and nine more movies.

I am in syndication and shown on movie nights, with other actors who died before their prime.

"Boyfriend," Tito says.

We are back on the porch. He has relit the cigar from the afternoon.

"Fred Lup," I say.

"Old Freddy Lup."

"Was he the guy from the meat shop?"

"No," I say.

"Good. Didn't like him."

Tito holds the cigar to my lips. I take a small puff.

"Fred Lup was my cable man, after I moved back to Kansas, after I was dead. He hooked everything up. He had a tattoo on his lower back. An arrow that pointed to his ass. His pants never rode down, but every time he bent over, his shirt would hike up, and I could see the arrow."

"You had to have him."

"When he was done, I told him he turned on more than my cable."

"And it was love."

"Sixty channels."

Puberty could only be delayed so long. I was seventeen. There were rumors. The accident was lucky for the studio. Afterwards I was approached by legal. They suggested that Ghostboy could die of complications, that we could part ways in peace. They offered financial compensation.

I would have continued acting as long they let me. I was willing to go on. But I could see how this was more fitting.

My career was easy to leave because I wasn't used to being famous anywhere but the set and publicity events — it took makeup and swarthy black fabrics to appear as Ghostboy.

Without experiencing my own celebrity, it's hard to miss it.

Fingers are different.

I was on the ladder, for a movie, reaching for a book. I was acting, had made myself forget that the book would flash. And then there was a hiss, light and corrosives, my fingers coming apart, disintegrating.

In a few seconds, I was less than I had been.

I could have had clamps and screws, a number of prosthetics. They wanted to take the whole hand and rebuild from there, but I didn't let them. I was used to having things beyond my control shape me. It felt cheap to replace anything. I had been too young to consciously grieve my parents or my childhood. After the accident, I probably felt like I deserved to fully experience my loss.

I did therapy and minimal surgery, but nothing reconstructive.

It was probably stupid. After about six months, I started regretting it, but have never changed my mind. For several years, I had a full staff to help me. Now I have Tito and Wellbutrin.

Still, I don't have fingers.

I was able to touch, to twist yarn around and behind my fingers, to knot my shoes, and than I wasn't. Without prosthetics, my fingers are a metaphor for the Internet, virtual sensation moving on electricity.

What I have grown to replace the fingers is suspicion. I don't miss the touching so much — I miss trusting it. Fingers are nothing if not loyal, a network of spies. When they return from the front with a description of silk or wet metal, there is no doubting the news. And now I can't be sure of anything.

But there are trade-offs.

I can sink my ghostfingers into walls, through a mirror.

I can reach outside a closed car window.

I can feel past our molecular shells, into other people.

I am permeable.

"Boyfriend," Tito says.

It is the morning, after breakfast and Tito's webpage update. We are in the kitchen, with coffee. I use both hands.

"Tim Vargus," I say.

"Ever go by Timothy?"

"No. I was on location, in South Bend, Indiana. He was a normal sixteen year-old kid. Except he had a paper route. He spent a lot of time watching the shoot, his bag slung over his shoulder."

"And you decided to make him yours."

"We mostly went on walks. He let me stuff papers in boxes."

"I bet."

"He had orange hair," I say. They stop to imagine.

It is about an hour before lunch.

Outside, Wellbutrin is busy with his kite.

Tito is on the phone, setting up a meeting to buy the next house.

I am alone with the box.

Again and again, I watch Ghostboy on the ladder.

I use my palm and thumb to move the mouse, clicking on sources and interviews, a coalition of tragic glances. Tito has included links to several biographies, fan pages, tributes, the official Ghostboy site.

The whole story.

INTERZONE

Despite the fact that Tito and I were born in Kansas, we are not from here. I've never felt like I was from anywhere. When my parents died, I was already a ward of Hollywood. I returned to Kansas after I met my own end only because I had inherited property and it seemed as far away as possible.

In restaurants and gas stations, we encounter people with a soft lilt to their voice, people who refer to themselves as Kansans, people who know exactly how a Kansan treats neighbors and makes pie crust. I've always wanted to believe that Kansans — or

Californians, or Washingtonians — exist and that they comb their hair in a unique way. I've wanted to believe that I was simply searching for the place where my mannerisms originated.

In the last few months, since hooking up with the others, I've started to believe that locals fake it. Accents are learned, street names memorized. Nine out of ten houses get cable, the Internet, the same news you get at your local doughnut shop, all the way down to the gossip about the naked dress the Johnson girl wore to the spring formal.

Kansas has no shortage of interesting dead people.

Still, we might have moved if we could've gotten one of Burroughs' other places, especially the winter home. That place, in Mexico, is now a monastery. They weathered Tito's maelstrom of offers and counter-offers. Marxist or not, I've seen him work money like a well-toothed saw, patient enough to let gravity take over. What he wants toppled, topples.

But the monks held their ground, and Tito refused to broadcast from a space we didn't own. "Master's tools," he said.

The house is in Lawrence.

It was Burroughs' office. It's a raised ranch, smug and sparse. Tight-weave brown carpet, off-white paint on the walls. Barely lived in. It would be fit for an investment banker if not for all of the phone jacks, seventeen of them, lined up one against another along the length of the hallway baseboard.

"Revolution is data," Tito says. Wellbutrin puffs his cheeks. The last chord in its port, they head to the basement where we will spend our day and a half.

Instead of following them, I kick off my shoes and pad around on the carpet. I make my way to the bathroom. I don't need to pee, but I flush the toilet with the palm of my hand to see it run. I turn on the shower with my elbow. I wash my hands and face before shutting it off. I manage to get the blinds open, and through the tiny window I watch the backyard. There is no grass or soil. It is not especially rocky, mostly long slats of clay. There is an old, plastic igloo and a chain on a spike that's been half-twisted into the ground. I watch for a while, wondering who inherited the dog. Perhaps it died before Burroughs.

I go to join the others.

Indirectly.

I open every closet, peer out of every window, flip every switch in the house. In the phone-jack room, one of the switches makes Tito swear from the basement. I turn it back on and go to the kitchen. I use my thumbs to open the oven. It isn't large, just wide enough for a small turkey. I rock back and forth on my heels, checking the floor for squeaks.

"Revolution doesn't wait," Tito yells from the basement.

"I've finished the preview," Wellbutrin says. He is more polite than Tito, but he means the same thing. From the beginning, it's been more important to me to see how the dead lived, to smell the tap for minerals, to see how quickly the shower steams up the bathroom mirror. Tito and Wellbutrin will do the same things I just did, but not until we get what we came for.

I flip a few more switches on and off and head to the laundry room.

It is not lost on me that, at the first house, I made them wait almost two hours.

"We are un-fettering, re-conceiving," Tito says with a verve that can be mustered only by a Marxist from suburban Kansas City, a multimillionaire before he graduated from high school.

"These are the master's tools," he says. "Trick them up and Burroughs' ass baboons will soon be flipping cars in Everywhere City." He gives us a wild, thumbs-up sort of gesture.

"May you remember everything," he says to the monitor, his lips a few inches from the screen. "May you choke on it," he says before pulling back into his chair.

We have started.

All three times now, there has been a strangeness to the beginning. Indelible as the move from private to public is, it feels like something. It's not like little hairs on the neck or goose flesh. Not like being watched. It's more like an extended version of seeing a photographer's flash and knowing that a split-second version of you has been recorded. Even though I am not on camera, I feel it again now, as we bring Burroughs' house to you in streaming video. It doesn't matter if you are watching. I can feel it, coming from the box, a frequency that only hums when we are sending.

Tito made his money in sound, though his parents had plenty to help him out. He dabbled in pirate stuff, at first, though he won't admit he liked the games, the stolen music, the free software. He won't admit he liked the money. "The material was just a metaphor for my sadness," he says of it.

Mostly, I think he's right. He was awkward and lonely at the right time. Solitude turned into deep study, which turned into money. Theory came after the money, Marx on the back of a software program and the company he formed and sold within nine months. He says he was developing the ideology early, getting bootlegs and cheat codes to poorer hands. "Even the program was about redistribution," he says. "Robin Hood in binary."

I don't buy it.

Still, the program was a kind of revolution. I really can't tell you what it does. All I know is that it works, fills the room with music, makes voice recognition work better. And that it spread like contagion. Rolling Stone did a piece on him, a snap shot before I knew him. I saw the picture, the same bone structure as now, but his skin was too pale. He hadn't found his revolution yet.

"Go to two," he says.

I watch him adjust our monitor.

His hands are so small, his fingers barely bone, as fragile as mine were.

Though I typically don't trust people who understand technology — they seem like the pharaoh's magicians, unable to see a plague for what it is — Tito is different. As he cracks his hands and his foot rattles against a table leg I think that I trust him because he seems as uneasy with the magic as I am.

Wellbutrin is dying for a cigarette. He hasn't said anything, but he's fidgety in his chair. He's closer to the box than I am, and though he is trying to focus on our slow tour of the place, he is scraping his knuckles in a self-conscious rhythm against the cinder-blocks next to us. He only acts like Tito when he wants to smoke. He hasn't had a cigarette in a long time, not since changing his name. I didn't know him then, but I imagine that he scowled more.

He is rocking from his hips. The musty smell of the unfinished basement isn't helping the craving. He is quiet, which isn't unusual, but his lack of attention is dense and listless.

"Change is amputation," I whisper. "I was thinking."

"You're wrong," Tito says.

"Explain," Wellbutrin says.

"I've changed like a grand total of three times," I say. "When I lost my parents, when I lost my job, when I lost my fingers. You're different than you were as a smoker. That's all. Change is loss."

"Plato's tautology," Tito says.

Wellbutrin smiles and puts a finger to Tito's lips.

"Surely," he says as he turns to me, "addition is change, every bit as much as subtraction."

"If you give me a suitcase," I say, "I've lost my need for a suit-case."

"And your tautology is half-empty," Tito says.

"Why does it matter?" Wellbutrin asks.

"Look at us," I say.

For a few seconds, they do. They make eye contact, search my face. Before long, we are silent again, looking at the monitor, at the virtual brown carpet, the virtual beige rooms above us, walls we could touch if we went upstairs.

"A surprise," Tito says. It is the first any of us have said for a few hours. "Check your silent silence," he says. He begins typing again, a stubborn bob to his head and hand. "I've given this a bundle of thought, twenty metaphors worth at least. We need a brand new lute for the data renaissance."

He grins at us, and keeps typing. A few minutes later, the monitor divides in two, one half for the video of the house, the other for a chat room.

"Good," says Wellbutrin. "Feedback."

"And back again," Tito says. "We have a screen name."

"For what?"

"For Bill. BUR_GHOST," Tito says. "The people's poltergeist."

"Conjecture," Wellbutrin says.

"You wanted control."

"I want an audience to know what to look for."

"So tell them."

"In the guise of a virtual medium."

"Exactly," says Tito. "Look. We're selling this. Bottom line. We want this place, this man, the facts of this man to be un-suppressed. If we want this to inculcate and swim, we need to put a spin on it."

"That's crass," says Wellbutrin. "The point was no spin. The

visuals are the spin. Not us. Not with puppets. We can watch the
chat, see what sticks and what doesn't. We can address mistakes
in my write-up. And next time."

"We need to sell it," says Tito. "Revolution must be sold. Every truth must be sold."

"I'm not a revolution," Wellbutrin says. "This was an important man."

"And he's dead. Think of us as Elysian tour guides. There is
Bill playing William Tell, cooking up a heavenly speedball, knuck-
ling up to a hand of bridge."

"We've got the house. If that's not interesting enough than
we're selling something we don't own."

"Of course it's enough. It's a good bullet. But it needs to be
fired."

"We said trust the houses."

"We need to pull the trigger."

"Trust the house."

"Sell the house."

For now, they have finished.

Tito has pushed his chair back a bit, so he can face Wellbutrin
straight on. Their hands are fists. Their necks are corrugated with
veins. Still, their knees are almost touching, their bodies squared.
Even in their anger, they are a closed system.

Usually, fame feels like televised surgery, like being explored with
close-captioned explanations and conjecture. For all three of us,
fame was more like a public X-ray of a second cousin. We're all
famous, but you wouldn't know it by looking.

You'd never spot Ghostboy in the yellow and orange dresses I
wear. Tito's name is no longer connected to the story swapped at
cocktail parties about some strike-it-rich Internet kid. Wellbutrin
was only in a band for two years. And he played bass. He might

as well have worn a mask on stage. He went to grad school afterwards, and was almost never recognized, even with a half-dozen
songs in heavy rotation on most radio stations. If I started singing any one of them, you could probably sing along.

Perhaps we are drawing attention to these houses, to names
that haven't been in the paper more than a few times since death,
because we feel a kinship. What we are doing here is probably the
equivalent of teaching self-defense classes after you've been at-
tacked.

"We'll do it," I say. My voice is fully Ghostboy, thick in my throat.
My right hand is through Wellbutrin, my left through Tito. They
are unaware of what I am feeling — not inside them, exactly, but
something invasive, something liquid.

"We should do it," I say.

"Of course we should."

"At best it's plagiarism," says Wellbutrin.

"If we do it right, he gets to speak again," I say. "If we do it
wrong, we get to."

"Listen to the dead girl."

Wellbutrin rubs his pants with the back of his hands. After a
minute of this, he stops and looks at me.

"Once," he says. "I'll go on once. Ten minutes."

"The revolution will be televised," Tito says. "Bring a Ouija
board."

Wellbutrin laughs. His hand lingers on Tito's sweater.

It is a nice moment, but I'm not finished.

"It will be me," I say. "I'll be Burroughs."

They turn to me.

"She's right," Tito says, letting go of Wellbutrin. "It should be her."

"But I know Burroughs."

"And she knows death. Listen to her voice."

"I know Burroughs."

"And she's an actor."

"But there's no script. It's not acting. It's going on as him. I can do it without infringing."

"And she can sell tickets. She's our hook, our mad barker with Bill for a megaphone."

I watch their exchange. Tito is sucking on Sweet Tarts, drinking a generic cola. Wellbutrin is still fidgeting.

"Why do you?" he asks.

I'm not sure what to tell him.

I've been thinking about my parents, how they died, how everyone who talked to me explained the mechanics of the situation. It was industrial sabotage, poison in a few hundred packets of water-soluble aspirin. Somehow, they had headaches on the same day, and their medicine came from the same batch. They were dead before I ate lunch — pizza burgers and fries — at school.

Everyone was kind. They were gentle but insistent. They wanted to make sure that I understood that my parents were never coming back. How it all works. They talked about God if I asked them to, but they didn't have the answers I was looking for.

"I've been asking the dead questions for a long time," I say.

"Our necronaut," says Tito.

"Okay," Wellbutrin says finally. "But keep it simple. Remember, Tito has to type what you say. Keep yourself out of it."

"Make it strange," says Tito.

"Just Burroughs," Wellbutrin says. He smiles at me. "We're not selling T-shirts."

"Nothing wrong with a Marxist fund-raiser."

"Undiluted," says Wellbutrin. "We stay undiluted."

Tito makes way, and I move closer to the box, next to Wellbutrin.

On-screen, an idle chat is happening, names with numbers and underscores. They are arguing about the colors of the house, the empty corners, what furniture would be the most fitting. I place Wellbutrin's dog-eared and frayed books in a pile and let my hands rest on them. They seem surprised when I sink my missing fingers deep into text.

"Nutters and screaming babies," I say. My voice is still mine but it moves nasal, not as resonant as usual. Tito types and keeps with me. Wellbutrin is smiling, I think. I know he is shaking his head but I will not look at him. I keep my fingers in the books, doing my best not to think.

"Scumbags and skaghounds," I say. "Take heed and dust off your good ear, my frisky princes, my bright-eyed litterbugs. Spoons out, my dirty fiends. The movie is about to begin. The plane will land blindfolded. Give me your salty eyeballs, my sweet Rasputins. Turn your eely tentacles to the base of the wall. These are my tin-cup telephones. I will babble and fart.

"Have I told you about the man who taught his asshole to talk? Yes? Too many times? How about the man who played his veins like a mandolin? When he went off the junk, after they scraped his perfectly dumb asshole so that he could shit again, he got fat, so fat that his veins made a terrible noise in all that goddamned blubber. He could flick them and change their flabby pitch. I always thought it sounded like beating a pile of sausage.

"At first, he only took his arm out at parties. It was a murderous sight. Him in the middle of a circle of skag vultures so up on junk they couldn't be sure he wasn't hiding a grand piano. They listened to the wretch, his good veins, and they were sure he was holding on them. He must have some good junk to get his veins so sickly. They ripped him apart.

"Do not think," I say, "Do not think, my dumplings, that because he was clean that he was anything but delicious."

Tito is laughing now but he keeps typing.

"When his friends were done, they let him play Carnegie Hall. On stage with his arm. Flapping and Flapping, chord changes, arpeggios. He was a master of the once-junky arm. And let me tell you, there wasn't a goddamn body in the house to hear him. He might as well have used his veins to hang himself. But he won't shut up about it. I got an itch for the south, I say to him, just to change the subject. And he says Bill, let me tell you about the time I played the hall. He talks and goddamn talks.

"And then, when he is tied up in old age, and his friends have shot themselves dead a dozen times, Loaf City remembers a kid who used to play his arm at Carnegie Hall. He only strums his veins for family these days, but all these yappers, all they talk about was how they never heard anything sweeter than the man who put his once-junky blood to music."

My voice is weaker now, but I keep going.

When my voice finally gives out, I settle back into my chair. I am not exhausted or sweaty. It did not feel like possession. I just have a headache, a fuzzy one, like playing chess too long.

I'm no more or no less scared than I was before we started.

Tito and Wellbutrin put their hands on my shoulders but they do not say anything. For a while, we read the chat-room. Vampgirl69 thinks I swore too much and went on too long. Not_dead_yet thought the whole thing was hysterical.

I watch the house.

I am looking for something to have changed. The windows are still dirty. The carpet is still brown, still without footprints.

THE LIVING

Like the first times, it is a comfort to move around the house, to go into the yard, to see a real horizon. But we are less exuberant about it. Our morning after is overcast, so humid the air smells like hot pennies.

Wellbutrin takes his kite out and comes back inside.

Perhaps it is odd that we don't say much about the broadcast, but we never do. The more I think about the events of the last few months, the less unusual they seem.

I am curious about what I said, but no more so than I am about what Tito and Wellbutrin did when, at midnight, I left them alone. In either case, it is more tempting to imagine than it is to analyze.

Tito and Wellbutrin seem as un-reflexive as I am. Perhaps it is the humidity. Or we are getting used to this. Either way, we have been staying inside. When they ask, I tell them boyfriends, and, together, we explore the place.

When we leave the house, Lawrence, Kansas is real.

There is space to navigate. It is possible to get lost. There is no refresh button, no back arrow. There is only a square of major roads — Iowa, 23rd Avenue, Massachusetts, Highway 59.

We are walking on Massachusetts, a pedestrian-friendly main street, a half-mile from the house. It is a busy place, one shop after another. There are specialty stores, plus-sized leather goods, out-of-print comic books. It is crowded. A man feeds coins into a pop machine. A woman walks her dog. She is in a sweater, the same color as my dress. Her makeup is perfect, her hair done for the day. Everyone on the street has dressed for the sun, impatient for it to return — girls in brighter dresses than mine, boys in ripe T-shirts.

Every arm I can see is dark and freckled.

"Ken Hackney," I say, just to say something. "I was sixteen, he was nineteen. He taught finger puppetry to children. His laugh was always a surprise."

The others don't say anything.

We do not shop or gaze. We do not trade pleasantries with people who say hello. Even Tito — with all of his talk of taking the average person from "mule to unmule" — even Tito does his best to ignore strangers.

"This place," says Tito. "is a colonized place."

"Just shops," Wellbutrin says. "Just America."

"This is why our revolution needs carnies and hucksters," Tito says. "If it comes from without, more like an invasion, no one would know what do with their holograms, their refrigerator magnets. This street is why revolution must work like e.coli, why it must be ingested, internalized."

"A lot of it is locally owned," I say. "They picket Starbucks here."

"And they are content with that," Tito says. "That's a concession, not a revolution. No skin is shed. The consumer still suckles the tit."

He does not end with a flourish but with a sputter, as if he was simply too confused to continue. We are at a busy corner that moves with the rhythms of a morning crowd. Watches are checked against a public clock. Cell phones are used. Shoes are double-knotted.

Somehow, among the fully living, it is easier to remember my parents. Though I've been thinking about them all week, it hasn't been the same. In our dead houses, memory has been like my tenth grade drivers' ed. textbook — no matter how hard I try to read, I end up skimming.

In our basements and closets, with the distractions of the box and whatever magic it is capable of, I have only been able to recall facts: what I had for lunch that day, the color of the hospital room, how the place smelled, how cold I was.

It was a year after we had moved to California.

Looking back, I know that they were starting to like the city. My father had found a good place to walk the dog. He had started taking me on Saturdays before I was due at a shoot. I probably hadn't understood that he had ever been unhappy, but I remember how good it felt when he let the dog off the leash. He chased it, while I chased both of them.

My mother had it easier because she liked her job. She was an accountant for a food bank. I remember how much less tired she seemed when she got home from work, how many times she told me to find a career that felt good, how many times she asked if I was okay doing horror movies, if I was happy putting on makeup and pretending to be dead.

Tito, Wellbutrin, and I have to walk single file. Other groups — louder and more confident than we are — don't move for us. The sun still isn't out. It will storm tonight, but for now it's just this heavy air, thick like static or a magnetic field. The street is broad and long, probably not as crowded as it gets at night, but everyone is so loud, their footsteps, their breathing. I find myself walking too cautiously, jerking away from anyone who gets close.

I wonder if phobias accrue over time.

My short hair is wet with sweat, my scalp tight with itching.

My finger-less hands are awkwardly clasped behind me.

Sometimes, when Wellbutrin is not caught up in his own anxiety, he reaches forward, and we walk like a two-car train. Tito is

in front, trying to get us where we are going as quickly as possible.

For a couple of years — longer than I have been with Tito and
Wellbutrin — the crowds have been like this, a sour wad in my
throat. I wonder if this is how Los Angeles felt for my parents,
before the dog park and food bank. I wonder if they felt invisible,
or too visible. I wonder if they were just lonely, something less
jumpy, less crazy-feeling than what I feel; this street, by all mea-
sure, is a nice place with friendly strangers.

I wonder if they had good reason not to like the city.

I wonder what they gave up to move there.

I know that, before they left for California, my parents thought
of themselves as locals. When I finally saw their bodies, both of
them were wearing Kansas University sweatshirts.

I am wondering why they agreed to move to Los Angeles in
the first place — why my chances at celebrity were enough for
them to give up Kansas — when Tito takes my arm and pulls us
into a restaurant.

In a corner booth, with an arc seat, we sit three in a row, touching at hip and shoulder. We are sweaty, out of breath. I feel stupid. I see the shape of Tito's mouth, how quickly Wellbutrin's
eyes are adjusting to the dark, empty sandwich shop.

If what I have is a phobia, perhaps it is viral.

The air conditioning is on too high, and the place is as cold as a
grocery store. I feel my skin tighten. My knee begins to shake
almost immediately. But the air is easier to breathe than outside.
The dim light is much easier to see through.

"What's it like to be recognized?" Tito asks. He is between
Wellbutrin and I, leaning his body on his elbows.

"Ask Wellbutrin."

"You were more famous."

"Yeah she was."

"But I wasn't spotted. Not unless I was in costume. Wearing black, and the hair, and you know. When it happened, I was playing a character."

"Same here," says Wellbutrin. "I was on stage. I saw the adoration and stuff, but it was part of a show. Every once and a while, someone stopped me and asked if I was who I was. But only the fanatics, and even they would have believed me if I said I had no idea who they were talking about."

As he talks about it he chuckles. He has talked of how tired he was in those days, touring and recording. But to see him remember it, after the name change and two degrees, is not to believe him.

"Say the name again."

"No," he says.

"Plato's dead, Baby," says Tito. His hands are touching Wellbutrin's. "Archetype is marketing scheme. My coffee maker is closer to Coffee Maker. My dog is more Dog."

"The hell does that mean?"

"Say the name again."

"Is," says Wellbutrin. "Are, Was, Were, Be, Am, Been, Has, Have, Had, Do, Did, Does, May, Can, Might, Must, Shall, Will, Should, Could, Would," he says. Not fast, not in the memorized list that I'm sure he first learned it. I have tried to say it back to him. I always get hung up at been. We know the rest of the story, but he continues with it, and we laugh in the usual places. "But no one wanted to know all that so we were just The Helping Verbs. Even that was too much for radio stations. The Verbs they said. Suddenly, our connotation included running, jumping, exploding."

"That's a sad, sad metronome," Tito says.

"What he said," I say.

Over Tito, Wellbutrin smiles at me.

It's true that I was more famous. I had to work crowds. Once, legal let me do a commercial in full makeup, selling mufflers — with Speedo your car can be dying and no one will know. I did voice-overs all the time, for commercials, for documentaries, an IMAX show about the Sahara and the cruelty of the natural world.

And while it's true that several people in this place would recognize Tito's story, or Wellbutrin's bass riffs, everyone here could describe my death.

Finished with lunch, we remain in the booth with emptied plates, scattered utensils. Wellbutrin is whistling, his softness restored. No one has mentioned the broadcast since we left the house. I have not heard any of his final verdicts about our act of appropriation, whether or not I violated his literary boundaries. I'd like to know.

Still, I don't want to say anything.

I decide to sit for awhile, our table cluttered but separated from the rest of the restaurant, but Tito grows anxious, getting his color back. For a while he just fidgets, rubbing his chin with a fist. I can hear his hand scraping against his beard.

Eventually, he begins to drum the table with a knife and spoon.

"We found our hook," he says.

"It went fine," says Wellbutrin. I am unsure how to read his tone of voice.

"More than fine," says Tito. "Better. Firecracker Bill, like a bulldozer."

"Sure," says Wellbutrin. He is growing heavier again, the same grace, but defeat in his voice. "This is dangerous."

"It played out."

"It did," he says. "But that's no guarantee it will again."

"Yeah it is," Tito says. "That she said anything is red-letter proof that she said it right."

"No it's not."

"Boys," I say. "Who's next?"

Whether or not we do the chat again, there is no question that there will be another house. Though money isn't an issue, we will put the estate up for sale, probably by the end of the week. We attempted to give our first, the Capote house, to charity. But it created a stir. If it happens in real space, exposure is not what we are looking for.

"Good question," Wellbutrin says.

"Browder," says Tito.

Wellbutrin laughs, and I have to smile as well.

Earl Browder was the head of the American Communist Party during World War II. Tito wanted to do him before Stafford. Wellbutrin had to stoop to saying things like "ideleonomics" to get Tito to hold off this long.

I know that he is crucial to Tito's ideology, but nothing we do, no amount of house footage, will make Earl Browder a personality. We might as well be shooting from the grave of a random uncle.

"He's not famous," I say.

"And he's not a writer," Wellbutrin says.

"Both troubles are really the pistons that will make us go, go, go," says Tito. He sits fully upright again, still shorter than both of us. He takes his hands from the table. He thumbs at his nose and rocks as he speaks. "People don't know him, true. We want a reformation of ocracy," he says. "And that can't happen only with writers. Browder needs us to make his bones sing. Burroughs, if you want to speak from a technical mouth, already sings from the page. Browder is as deserving as anyone."

He quiets. When we don't say anything, he begins to tap his knife against his water glass.

"Look," he says, still tapping. "We're ready for this, for him. After Ghostboy, we have the base audience, several hundred hits since last night. We're ready for the next step, ready to bring fame to a figure instead of the other way around. And we can start to bring out the heavy boxes, pry open the crates marked politics."

"But politics is all he is," says Wellbutrin. "Nothing needs to be clarified. People want to know Browder, they can take a class on the cold war."

"People can take a class on anyone," Tito says. "If that brochure is accurate, then we're selling obsolete swampland. Browder's as much of an enigma as anybody. Plus, he's close. Who else we got left in Kansas?"

"We can leave Kansas."

"I bought the estate," says Tito.

"Was it even for sale?"

"I bought it."

"You bullied whoever lived there into leaving."

"I increased our offer. They decided it was worth it. I'm just playing their game, revolution as a slow poison. I signed electronically. We pack up and go. We can be there by sundown tomorrow."

He's right. With money, the world is smaller. As I watch the waitress ring up our ticket, I am ashamed of how small ours has become.

Earl Browder probably was the first and only American Marxist, the one who saw how the system had to adapt if it wanted to work here. He very well might have something to teach us, even Wellbutrin and I. But he doesn't have a story. For most of our audience, whoever you are, no narrative would animate the house. We could tell you, but you'd have no way of knowing if we were honest. None of it would sound familiar. It would just be a house.

We would have to add Browder's name to your consciousness.

Tito would say this is exactly what we are doing: un-erasing.

I'm not so sure.

He leads us back along Mass. Our dissension is giving him quicker steps and more swagger. He wears a lofty smirk. He knocks self-righteously on shop windows and tears flyers from telephone poles.

"Un-dissemination," he says. "Cleaning up consumer pollution."

A similar looking crowd to the one that ignored us on the way to the restaurant is more attentive this time. A woman in a torn army jacket stops to watch Tito. She is not the only one. Tito holds himself as tall as he can. When he sees the strip of chain stores that lie just beyond the confines of downtown, he begins shouting.

"This is the den of corruption and greed," he says. Wellbutrin and I fall back.

This won't last long.

Tito is deep into a rant about factory education. He accuses a few students of majoring in "consumer studies." He tips over a garbage can. There is a crowd forming. I am not sure if they are listening to him. Some of them look thoughtful, but there is another vibe to the whole thing, as if Tito were a street performer.

Before his lecture is over and the crowd thins, there is almost ten dollars in singles and change lying at his feet.

"The people are ready," he says when he returns to us.

Wellbutrin puts a hand on Tito's lower back and whispers, his head right next to Tito's ear. Tito nods but doesn't seem to agree as he whispers back.

Whatever is exchanged, I can't hear it. Soon we are walking again.

Tito shrugs Wellbutrin's hand from his back.

His mouth is a knot of lips.

Wellbutrin hangs back by me.

We leave Massachusetts.

The clouds are finally threatening rain, probably in a few minutes.

A block ahead of us, a bicyclist is hit by a car.

Tito gets there first. By the time Wellbutrin and I catch up, he is helping a man of about forty. There is blood. I am uncertain what to do. I lean closer to the man, close enough to smell him. The man's arm is twisted beneath him. I am able to get it free, but I can't figure out how to straighten it. I know it should look some other way. I try to use Tito's as a model, to remember how a body works. The man catches me, or at least looks at me.

When he smiles he is bloodier, missing teeth.

I put his arm down.

Wellbutrin has busied himself with the bike. He has it on the grass, bending over it, tugging at its chain, trying to straighten the cross bar. Based on the way he is breathing, he is more frightened than he is concerned.

"It's okay," the man says to Tito. "You didn't see me."

"We weren't driving," Wellbutrin says. He is insistent and hard.

"Could have happened to anyone," says the man.

"We weren't driving," Wellbutrin says, shouting.

"Sir," says Tito, surprisingly steady. "We were walking behind you. We weren't in the vehicle that hit you."

"Who was?"

"They drove off."

The man does not like this. He breathes in angry, flustered breaths. He seems to bleed faster.

"Call the police," he says. "Tell them the license number."

I look at Tito and Wellbutrin. They shrug.

"You need an ambulance," I say.

He looks at me, a little shaken by my voice.

"Am I dying?"

"I don't know," I say.

He thinks about it.

"Call the police," he says.

Wellbutrin looks useless, but he realizes that the errand is a way to leave. He tries to figure out where the closest phone is, pointing in a few directions, mouthing something to himself.

He gives up, running through an alley.

Waiting, I can't stop looking at the man's bloody mouth. He has managed to sit against the curb. I don't think he should have been moved, but it's been so long since I read anything about first aid. Tito has managed to stop some of the bleeding with his shirt.

Topless, Tito is not unattractive. Looking at him, I remember that he ran track in high school and that he is younger than Wellbutrin and I. Somehow, without the shirt, he is not as skinny as he is in clothes. He sits next to the man, listening. He seems uncomfortable, but nods when he is supposed to, even going so far as to touch the man's shoulder once or twice.

To look at the man — the places in his gums that held teeth less than twenty minutes ago — is to remember his accident. As we wait for Wellbutrin and the police, it happens again and again in front of me. The car clips his front tire. The man lurches into the air. His head hits the hood. Knees and elbows twirling.

The police arrive before Wellbutrin. They ask questions Tito and I can't answer. We didn't think of looking for a license plate. I tell them that I froze because of the intensity of the accident. I don't tell them that, as soon as it started happening, I wanted to run away.

I wish we hadn't seen it.

I am resentful of how I keep seeing it, how his bloody smile stays with me. It seems unfair to be involved in something like this when we so clearly do not belong out here.

When the cops have disappeared and the man has been taken away, we return to Burroughs' house. Without speaking, we move to the basement. Without the box on, it is too dark to close the door. Wellbutrin has his hands on his face. Tito is trying to smile at me. For him, he seems calm.

"Browder then," he says.

"Yes," says Wellbutrin. "The sooner the better."

"Ghostboy?"

I nod.

Tito gets up. He puts his hand on Wellbutrin's shoulder for a moment, before leaving the room. He returns with pretzels.

"We are commotion," he says, standing in the doorway.

"Yes we are," Wellbutrin says faintly, muffled by his hands.

"Agamemnon in megabytes."

"Yes we are."

For the first time since we got together there is no dissent, no questions for the sake of clarity. When Tito sits, he sits on Wellbutrin's lap, twisting his fingers into Wellbutrin's hair.

"Browder," I say, letting my voice do what it will.

"Say it again," says Tito. "Let me hear it."

"Browder."

"Say a revolution in data."

"A revolution in data."

"Say the dead walk."

"The dead walk."

"Settled," says Wellbutrin, and I can tell that it is. Tito turns on the box. Online, he finds a recipe for braised beef tips. He emails the recipe and a credit card number to a Lawrence grocery store that will deliver.

Later in the afternoon, while the others pack, I wander. My last hours in these houses are nothing like my first. When we got here, I was looking to see how our predecessors might have lived. Now, I try to get a good look at exactly what we are leaving.

I sit on the carpet.

I look out the back windows as the rain comes in.

I kick at the phone jacks along the baseboard.

I listen to doors, bedrooms and closets, my ears pressed firm against the wood.

I touch the corners of every room, investigating the paint.

The others are in the basement, almost finished. Without the cameras, there is an uneasy peace. Up here, there is no noise. If the house is shifting I cannot hear it.

It occurs to me that the house is pretty much just a house. We came here for ghosts, and I think we found one, but perhaps we brought it with us. Perhaps there is no difference between ghosts and ghost stories.

I go into the back yard, where the rain is.

I investigate a windmill.

It is on a white pole and made from bicycle tire. Around the rim, funnels are glued to catch the wind, painted in alternating primary colors. It is the only thing that wasn't removed or disconnected when Burroughs died.

I watch it twirl until the light is completely gone.

A New Manifesto

We are in Tito's van, heading west.

Traveling always impresses me — distance is comforting.

Even if there is no real difference between places, the affectation of being local is only possible because of distance. It is one reason I distrust the box. I appreciate the magic of teleportation, but there is a romance to the in-between.

It is good to drive.

Soon, we are far enough away from anyone that the natural world becomes accessible. Tito asks to take the next exit. Wellbutrin does. We drive along the county road for a few blocks, until it comes to a T. Both directions are gravel. We stop. There is no brook, no grove of trees, no animals. One direction is a wheat field, the other black, freshly tilled soil. It is the natural world at its most commonplace and cultivated, but we all leave the van.

When Wellbutrin and Tito walk along the gravel road, talking in tones I can't hear, I decide to set out by myself.

The air smells good.

The field is inviting, full of light.

It takes a while, several minutes, but eventually I am deep enough that the way I came is identical to every other direction. I am completely alone. No one can hear me shout. I run my hands through the wheat. I lie down to trace cloud shapes. Every few minutes, the sky looks like a new sky.

The ground is damp. The sun is hot on my cheeks, on the skin of my nose, in the phantom firings of my missing fingers. I hear insects and feel something crawling near my sock.

If I were watching the clouds on the box I would be more comfortable, air-conditioned in a lumbar-friendly chair. Still, I don't move for the insects, don't wipe sweat from my forehead, don't get up until I imagine the others waiting.

When I get back to the van Tito and Wellbutrin are already there. Tito is looking for something on the ground. Wellbutrin has his shirt off. He was stung by a bee, on his chest.

"We were dancing," he says.

The sting is puffy and pink, the shape of a comma. I poke it with a thumb and he flinches. Tito finds a small rock. With it and a fingernail he goes to work, trying to remove the stinger.

"Got to get it out," he says. "Revolution of pus."

"That's not funny," Wellbutrin says.

He is shaking, his shoulders pale and round. He does not make eye contact with either of us until Tito has finished and his shirt buttoned.

"I'll drive again," he says.

Back on the road, Tito sings union songs, playing a banjo from behind us. I have my hand out the window. As we glide along the paved strings between one here and the next, the wind pushes at me.

I can feel the space we move through.

When Wellbutrin asks me to close the window so he can hear Tito playing, the afternoon is reduced to a picture of itself.

The Browder place is good-sized, two stories.

Tito finds a key in a hollow fixture outside.

As soon as he opens the door, it is clear that he must have offered a lot of money, enough that whoever was living here was willing to leave in a hurry. There are more signs of occupancy than there are to the contrary. The floors are hardwood, recently waxed. There are pictures on the walls, furniture in the rooms. There are bowls for pet food, labeled Buffy and JoJo. The bathroom is decorated with sailboats and pictures of kittens. There is food in the refrigerator, a diploma on the wall of the third bedroom.

"We own this place?"

"Yeah," says Tito. I can't tell if he is annoyed. He wants to get the cameras up tonight, so we have plenty of time for the write-up in the morning. He obviously notices all of the consumer trappings, but does his best to seem unperturbed.

"We start upstairs," he says.

Wellbutrin and I follow him. The room he leads us to is blue, covered with basketball players. The wallpaper is Nike.

"Nothing gets touched," says Wellbutrin.

"We can't do it like this," Tito says. He sits on the bed.

"Rules," Wellbutrin says. "Boundaries."

"This was to be a stronghold," Tito says. "The place where our mantra became crystallized, a blowtorch in the hands of the people. It can't be a commercial for tennis shoes."

"I'm not a revolution."

"I am."

"You said American Marxism was sly capitalism."

"This isn't sly."

"Than you need to show it, and hope the people react the same way you did. They need to want to take the posters from the wall."

"This one is mine," he says, running his hand along the wall, picking gently at a corner of one of the posters. "This is my important man."

"Then let him go as he's been left," says Wellbutrin.

"They weren't relatives."

"The space is the space."

"The space is cluttered. Not the space at all." He is on the edge of the bed, his body limp. His words seem to fall out of him.

"This clutter, this stuff, is the mask, the static, the blindfold that must be lifted."

Wellbutrin sits down, next to Tito. He pulls Tito into his chest, running his hand through Tito's hair. He looks up at me, thoughtful and scared.

"If we move one thing, what's to stop us?"

"Maybe we don't need to be stopped," Tito says.

"Ghostboy?"

"It's a temptation," I say. "If we do it in the right spirit."

Tito hasn't moved. His head is still in Wellbutrin's armpit.

Despite being wrapped into each other, and keeping the discussion entirely theoretical, the atmosphere is that of a lovers' spat, like it could easily turn into who always does what, who never makes time, who is emotionally schizophrenic.

"I can go either way," I say before leaving them to figure it out.

I explore the bedrooms before ending up in what must have been the kids' bathroom. It connects two rooms. Tito and Wellbutrin are on the other side of one of the doors, but I can't hear anything. After peeing and washing my hands I look through the drawers. There are bottles of expired antibiotics in one, toothpaste and floss in another.

Next to the sink there are two sonic toothbrushes, plugged in, their on-buttons glowing.

I want to try.

The toothpaste has a flip top and tastes like licorice.

Sound is supposed to remove the plaque — it hums loudly — but the brush shakes so hard that I have to use two hands. When it hits a tooth with anything other than the bristles, the noise rattles my mouth. It doesn't hurt exactly, though all the vibrating is making my missing fingers ache nostalgically.

The brush is used, of course, and I hope I don't have to explain myself to Tito or Wellbutrin. I'm not afraid of germs, though it's interesting to contemplate what might be on the brush.

I imagine a six year old girl, dark hair like mine. She likes to wear necklaces made of candy. She collects frog stickers. She likes to wear yellow. Until recently, she brushed her teeth every night in this mirror. When she listens to music, she thinks the bands actually live in the CD. She thinks that Muppets are real because she has seen them eat.

None of the rooms in this house have been decorated for her, but I can believe that I am using her toothbrush. It is easy to see her in the mirror, the exaggerated way she opens her mouth. I can hear her humming along with the toothbrush, the way I am now.

When I finish, I move to the living room and wait for the others. Some time later, they come down. It is clear that Wellbutrin has conceded, but that neither he nor Tito knows exactly what the concession is.

"We need boxes," Tito says.

It takes a few minutes, but we find several flattened and shelved in a supply room off the attached garage. Wellbutrin and I struggle to put them together. Immediately, Tito takes three and heads back into the house. Without fingers, I am better suited to hold flaps in place while Wellbutrin uses tape to make things sturdy.

"Will ten do?" he asks.

"I really don't know," I say.

"This is just cleaning, right?"

We are both squatting on the concrete, leaning together, over a now-finished box. This close, his eyes are a slightly different color. I expect to find sadness in his face, and it's there, but there's another quality too, an anxiousness, like we're trying to get away with something. I feel it too.

"We should help him," he says.

"We should," I say, but we don't get up, and the moment changes.

We linger, our faces close enough that I can smell his breathing, a little sour, but not unpleasant. I put my hand on his soft chin and smile weakly. He touches my hand with his own.

The contact is conspiratorial. Looking at him looking at me, I become aware — or see clearly — that Tito's absence is not merely a function of his not being here. He is working at a different speed, for different reasons, than Wellbutrin and I are. He probably has been for some time. Maybe all along.

He doesn't need us.

When we get up, Wellbutrin and Tito will continue to be what they have always been. They will touch, and probably go to bed together. But I know now that Wellbutrin and I share something — a curiosity, a fear, a dependency — that Tito moves too fast to understand.

Putting things — trophies, canned goods, all of it — in boxes brings about a different kind of contact with the house than I have experienced so far. More than Tito and Wellbutrin, I have poked around the places we have owned. But, other than when Wellbutrin has made meals, none of us has interacted with the houses as functional spaces. Even camera installation has treated the houses as dead, empty rooms.

We have not had to make room for things, look under beds, or gather loose items from corners and closets. I feel like I understand the wrinkles and limitations of this space in a way that, with the first properties, I was only guessing.

Wellbutrin is working like I am, paying as much attention to the house as he is to the items he gathers. When he looks at me, he smiles. When he looks at Tito, he seems on the brink of saying something.

Tito isn't bothering to find places to stow the goods, content for now to fill boxes, one after the next. There is an efficiency in his movements, as if his mind and his body are finally working at the same blistering pace. He is graceful. He jumps to take things off of a shelf that should be too tall for him. He balances an armload and pivots to his box. When it is more convenient, he throws, never missing.

"Boyfriend," says Wellbutrin.

Tito doesn't stop. If he listens, or disapproves of Wellbutrin's timing, he doesn't give any indication.

"Mickey Fundus," I say. I wait for a wisecrack, but most of the jokes in the old boyfriend game come from Tito. Wellbutrin puts a couple of board games into his box sideways, so they stick out of the top. He is chewing on the syllables of the name, as if I had recommended a chiropractor.

"He was in acupuncture," I say. "When I was shooting *The Last Train Leaves Early,* I sprained my ankle. He was called in to get the swelling down. He figured out the gender stuff when one of the needles needed to go into my knee. He said I had girls' knees. I asked him out, and we went to a drive-through. A space movie. Our only date."

I wait for anyone of a number of jokes but none come. Tito is taking down a gaudy clock. Wellbutrin is looking in his box, deep in imagining.

Eventually, we have enough boxes that they are in the way. Tito isn't willing to give up another room to storage. He and Wellbutrin have moved the furniture to the supply room off the garage. He wants the house to seem big and complicated, lots of nuance, completely empty.

For a while, Tito tries to find ways to hide the boxes, one or two at a time, in rooms we will be shooting. He looks for off-camera corners and closets we can afford to keep closed. Wellbutrin and I are willing to help, but Tito doesn't let us know how. He paces and flexes his hands. Occasionally he hops up and down, as if he were trying to keep his feet warm.

"Think," he says.

He has not said a single incomprehensible thing since the decision was made. Watching him rub his chin, he strikes me as an alternate version of himself. Even as pulls at one ear while fiddling with the zipper of his sweatshirt, something he always does, he seems different. I wonder if his mood — this solitude and purpose — is completely new for him, or if this was what he was like before us.

He exhales loudly, self-consciously, shaming us for not thinking as hard as he is.

Eventually he gives up and decides we will have to keep the boxes with us. He picks up two boxes and heads for the Nike bedroom, where we will be staying during the broadcast.

Wellbutrin and I follow, one box each. Tito does not wait. Before we have dropped our stuff, he is going back downstairs for more, despite the fact that we have boxes in every room. I'm not sure they will all fit, but Tito moves so fast that questions would be mutiny. Wellbutrin and I, in unspoken consensus, stick to fetching boxes on the same floor as the bedroom.

Without fingers, my hands are unsteady. My boxes need to be light. It is hard to tell, just looking, if I will be able to manage. It's not a question of strength but of leverage. I can get most of them into the air, before they begin to topple one way or the other, and Wellbutrin needs to lurch over and help me get them back down.

"Boyfriend," he says, the third or fourth time I pick up the same, awkward box. "One from after the accident," he says. I smile at him, as I try a new box and manage to keep it from tipping.

"How do you know I'm not out of those?"

"You're never out," he says.

"I'd rather tell you about Squid Lawson," I say, starting toward the bedroom. "He played hockey, goalie, for a men's team in Kentucky. His real name was Jay. If they didn't call him Squid, they called him Kentucky Jay. He was only sixteen, they were all thirty. They were the only team he could play for, the only team in Louisville. I met them all shooting *Stranger Death*. Something about how he played, how reckless he was, I don't know. We never had sex, but we kissed a lot, ate lunch together for several weeks. I'm not positive he was straight."

We go back and forth, piling up boxes, along the wall. I hand them to Wellbutrin so he can get them high, but the boxes don't stack well, odds and ends sticking out.

I am not sure what will happen to all of it when we sell the place.

I imagine the family, the girl with black hair.

I know they gathered everything they thought they would regret leaving, that they have enough money — thanks to Tito — to replace the rest. But there is the diploma, the trophies, several books of photos. Surely, we have as many of their keepsakes as they do. I wonder if they will regret leaving so fast, if they will buy new evidence of their past, try to replace scrapbooks and ribbons from first-grade wrestling tournaments.

When the boxes have all been gathered, we barely have enough space left to set up the computer. Luckily, the bedroom is attached to the bathroom so Tito's toilet stays in the van. When we start broadcasting, we will share the bed.

For now, I am trying to sleep in it.

It is far more comfortable than my bedroll, but it could be softer.

I'm not sure what's happening in the room next to mine.

I only have lurid conjecture. Noises and muffles.

After we finally got the cameras installed, Tito finally stopped pacing. For the first time all night, he could see us again, especially Wellbutrin. He stared at him, at the loose form of his body. For his part, Wellbutrin seemed eager to accept whatever Tito was offering.

I don't hear them all the time, just an occasional thump and giggle. If these were not my last hours alone for almost two days, I would consider investigating. I would fetch something from the kitchen before creeping up to their door.

As it is, I am more interested in myself.

For a while, when I lost the fingers, I was sexless.

Eventually I became less interested in other bodies, more compelled by the details of my own.

Tonight, I imagine floating on a sea of hands.

I wake up to Tito rummaging through boxes at the foot of my bed.

"Morning," he says, smiling. He is no less efficient than last night, but he is somehow less aggressive. He picks up items, one after the next. Most end up back in boxes.

Though there is less of a path to the door than there was before I fell asleep, I am able to get to the bathroom where I wash my face with soap and use the black-haired girl's toothbrush. She is in the back seat of a car, running her tongue over her teeth. She is unused to them feeling filmy, so slick. She uses a hand to smell her breath. She is half-disgusted, ashamed that it is coming from her mouth, but she doesn't stop smelling it, cupping her hand every few miles.

Her name is Theresa.

I am sure of it.

She is on her way to California.

Back in the bedroom, Tito is still sitting, cross-legged in front of a box. He holds a pocket watch, weighing it, testing the strength of its chain, before setting it aside.

"What are you doing?"

"I changed my mind," he says. "The house needs ethos."

He winks at me. It is a literal gesture, without irony, unlike anything I have seen from him. It is clear that he will not give a further explanation. I am guessing that he no longer wants the house completely empty, that he wants a few items strategically arranged — the pocket watch, a pair of binoculars, things he is putting into a pile — stuff that defines its owner as being having varied, worthwhile interests.

"But Browder didn't live here last," I say. "This stuff isn't his."

"No one knows anything about him," he says. He is almost polite. "You've all but said so. No one knows he didn't leave it exactly like this. If we are remembering a person no one remembers, there is no photograph to compare against the picture we draw."

He picks up an antique flask. He sniffs it before adding it to his pile of keepers. He gets up smoothly, a sort of twist without using his hands, and moves to trade his box for another. When he sits down again, and gets it open, the box is full of books. He takes them out, one after the next, flipping through them, knocking dust off against his pants.

"He wouldn't have read any of this," he says.

"Where's Wellbutrin?" I ask.

"Downstairs," he says, "painting the office."

I go find him.

The room is about ten by sixteen with a simple square window that shows the highway. A large, wooden desk — faded towards orange — has been pushed into the center of the room from a corner where the carpet is still flat.

Wellbutrin is on a stepladder, painting a single wall pink.

I want to ask him how Tito talked him into it, but he is moving so smoothly that I suspect he no longer objects. Watching — the long, vertical motion of his roller, the little snap of his wrist at the top and bottom of each pass — I realize that the room was his idea.

I would like to decorate Theresa's room in yellow. I know we don't have time, and Tito wouldn't go for it. Still, I would like to put daisies in a glass vase on the windowsill. I would like to leave her favorite animals on the bed. If by some miracle she were to see the broadcast, I would like her to know we have not forgotten.

As always, we start at noon.

The house looks like our other houses, abandoned, stripped down.

Like the others, it is haunted if you want it to be.

There is no evidence of tampering. The lack of dust only serves to bring the place's sterility into greater focus. The pocket watch, left on the kitchen counter, seems completely orphaned.

We are the difference.

Tito isn't twitchy. He watches the chat room. Though he worked carefully on the write-up, adding resonance to the scattered objects and pink wall, he doesn't leave anything to the reader. He has logged on as a random observer, someone from Saskatchewan, who happens to know a great deal about the dead Marxist. When the conversation strays, he sits up a little taller but doesn't panic. He types carefully.

Wellbutrin and I watch the house, but we don't defer to it, not like before. We talk loudly — sometimes about the broadcast, sometimes not — like what we're seeing is no more fragile than television.

"Boyfriend," he says.

"Clifford Pit," I say. "He never went by Cliff, for obvious rea-sons. He sold ice cream in Branson, Missouri. The only vacation I ever took. This girl I knew, the female lead in *Fear Helix*, she talked me into coming, but didn't see me for two days after we stopped for a frozen yogurt. He never knew I was who I was."

Wellbutrin nods.

"I kept his number for two years, but never called."

"No, no," Tito says. "Capital doesn't work like that."

I look at him.

He types so calmly that it is hard to remember that it is him.

I don't want to approve of what he is doing. I've always thought that history is a Rorschach test, the years like dark curls. When I was BUR_GHOST, I was still trying to be part of history's inky shape.

Watching Tito taking the guesswork out of it, it seems as though we have been doing it all along, choosing the houses, writ-ing our blurbs, posing as ghosts in one way or another.

Looking at the house we've reshaped, how the sunlight falls across a pair of cufflinks on the floor of an otherwise empty mas-ter bedroom, I realize that what I wanted — an alive past, com-forting and vital — is impossible.

Though I've always suspected conspiracy, I'm in on the secret now.

"Boyfriend," Wellbutrin says.

We have about forty minutes to go. I am more tired than I've been at the end of a broadcast. Part of it is that we are on a bed, without any back support, and I can't lie down.

"Tatoskins Johnson," I say. "He was tall, with a wolf tattoo on his calf. At restaurants, he only ordered appetizers and desserts. Once, we danced on a rowboat in the middle of pond. He never pretended like he was going to throw me in."

"Quiet," says Tito. In the light from the box, he doesn't look angry, though it is one of the first things he has said to us. "We do the last few minutes in silence," he says. "I've put an end to the chat. For now."

We do as told.

I don't watch the house.

From the start, I have known it better than our earlier houses.

By now, it holds no mysteries for me.

I can't say the same for Tito.

He is not particularly rapt, or reverent.

He is proud.

"I won't be long," Tito says to Wellbutrin. He says it warmly, but I don't know how much warmth gets through. The cameras are off, the house completely quiet. Tito looks up briefly from the chat he has restarted.

"Wake me," Wellbutrin says.

They kiss.

It is the first kiss they have allowed themselves in front of me. I suspect I only saw it because it wasn't a real a kiss but something else. I touch Wellbutrin, briefly, before he makes his way through the boxes of abandoned belongings to the hallway.

I wait for Tito to finish. I half lie down, propping my head on a hand, my elbow bent. I am drifting off, but Tito clicks away. The bed is firm and shakes gently with his keystrokes. I can't stop imagining his typing. It is lucid and clear but just out of reach. I am back in the wheat field, his words in the clouds. I am in a crowded elevator, sweating out whatever phobia I am cultivating, when the building starts to shake — in my panic I can hear a series of clicks, an old friend trying to show me the way out in a language I can't decipher.

When I fully return to the bedroom, I feel the strain in my wrist.

I am not sure if my phantom fingers are falling asleep or waking up.

My tongue feels large in my mouth, my teeth the wrong size.

Tito is still at it.

"You could keep Wellbutrin company," he says.

I get up clumsy and nauseated. I can't stop thinking, but am unsure what I am thinking about. I know I am chilly, that I want to lie down. In his dim light, I think Tito is someone else, a man I saw on a bus once, or in a deli.

"Where's Tito?"

"Go check on Wellbutrin."

I am not satisfied with the answer, but I do as he says.

When Wellbutrin sees that it is me opening his door, he sits up. I climb on the bed mat, and he relaxes into my shoulder, sliding his arm under my neck. I can tell by his touch that he is disappointed I am not Tito.

Still he tries to muster as much comfort as he can.

I am in my own bed, aware enough to know I have been moved.

I am alone, though the computer still hums.

For a while, like I did with Tito's typing, I take the sound into my dreams. I am chasing a white dog that never barks but sings in a fan-like voice. I am on a propeller airplane, over an ocean, surprised by how high we are, how quiet the ride is. I am on an escalator that never stops climbing.

Eventually, light comes through my window.

I pull myself awake. Outside, a few blocks away, in front of the closest house, a family gets into a sedan. They look ready for church. Even this far away, through the glass, they make me nervous.

It is the same thing I felt in Lawrence.

Unlike my fear of death, I can't remember when this fear started.

Without an origin, it is unpredictable. I worry that Tito, or even Wellbutrin, could someday make me feel this way — a fast throat and stomach, a sense of rising or falling way too fast.

The others are not awake, and I am tired of the room, so I go to the kitchen.

One of the items Tito set up for the broadcast was an old toaster. I plug it in and get bread from the refrigerator. When it pops up, I take the toast with my thumbs. The heat is enough to feel in my missing fingers, but I don't drop either piece. I struggle with knives, so I use a thumb, dipping it into a tub of butter, scrapping it onto the hot toast.

I have nothing to do but eat and wait.

Listening to the house, in the poorly-lit kitchen, I realize that — as well as I thought I knew it — I don't know any of its noises. It's been a long time since I lived in a truly familiar house, where I knew, without thinking, how to get the shower just right, whether the toilet would run if I didn't jiggle the handle.

I manage to pour myself some orange juice. The glass is plastic, one of the four we've been taking everywhere. It has several animated animals, two cats and a dog. I think it is a fast-food promotional, from a movie I saw as a child.

I imagine Theresa on her way to California, drinking from a similar glass, different animals, different movie. Her parents are listening as she explains why she likes the parrot best, why the bulldog is friendlier than anyone notices.

They know why she is between homes.

They can tell her.

If she worries that she won't make friends, they can reassure her. If she starts to cry, her mother will frown from where she is driving. If she starts to cry, her father will turn to her, over his seat.

His face will be like my father's, but alive.

THE DEAD

Only a few hours after waking up, Tito closes the deal on an unusual three-bedroom house in Emporia, Kansas. He gets up from the box and nods at us. Without his usual pep talk, or even so much as a word, he begins to pack.

I'm not sure exactly how we agreed to buy the place. It happened quickly. I was surprised, at first, when Wellbutrin said that if were willing to alter the house, we might as well alter the history.

Tito liked the idea. He seems to think he can start his revolution by convincing the public that it has been happening for years.

I'm not sure why I agreed.

Nonetheless, in less than an hour we bought the home of Sarah Pratt-Tipkins. We had no trouble finding the place because she's never owned it. As far as I know, the Sarah Pratt-Tipkins we're interested in — a staunch Marxist who wrote seven books of poems and starred in a half-dozen monster movies — never lived anywhere.

In the van again, we are driving north on the Kansas turnpike. The man who gave us the toll ticket when we got on a few miles ago was the first stranger we had talked to, in person, for several days.

Tito is driving with his new — or former, I'm still not sure — capacity for concentration. One finger is tapping a rhythm against the steering wheel.

In the distance, on top of the largest hill in sight, is a cross made of dark wood. I seem to remember my mother telling me, on our way to California, that the cross is older than the highway,

that it doesn't mark anything, that it was just a landmark for driving cattle.

"See that," I say, pointing.

"Sure," Tito says.

"Got it," Wellbutrin says from behind us, his voice slow.

"Years ago," I say, "before this was paved, there a was town up
there. Lincoln, Kansas. Not a big town, a thousand people or so."
I pause for questions but no one says anything.

Wellbutrin is looking at the cross.

Tito keeps us perfectly steady.

"Anyway, the place was hit by a tornado. Something like half
the people died. It's just a cemetery now, with a cross, so you can
see it from the highway."

"A whole town," Wellbutrin says.

"Half of it," I say.

Tito looks at me briefly.

"All at the same time," Wellbutrin says.

"Five hundred people dying at once," I say. "Together."

"Terrible," Wellbutrin says.

They are imagining it.

I imagine it too.

The Pratt-Tipkins house is my favorite so far.

Before Tito bought it, it had only been on the market a few
weeks. The man who lived here did some remodeling. He took
good care of the place. It is smaller than our other houses, two
rooms on the main floor, another in the basement. Still there is
an elegant fireplace, more than enough closets, and an efficient
floor plan. The dining room has a twelve-foot ceiling that creates
an unexpected largeness.

The living room has a multi-paned west window so that, during the first evening of our broadcast, light splays across the hard

wood floor in five, soft fingers.

Off of the kitchen is a bay window. We removed wallpaper, and repainted, to distinguish the nook from the rest of the room. Though of course the table is long gone, looking at the kitchen as the sun comes up, you can imagine Sarah Pratt-Tipkins separating a grapefruit, listening to the birds outside, memorizing lines, reworking a poem about workers at the Hutchinson battery plant.

On the website, Tito has included excerpts of several of Sarah Pratt-Tipkins's most famous poems, from all of her major periods, the early experiments with form, her later adherence to a deca-syllabic line, and, of course — relatively late in her career — her practically religious conversion to Marxism.

We wrote the poems together. We did excerpts, mostly, so that we didn't have the obligation of starting or ending anything. If you don't understand them, there are missing, unwritten stanzas that you probably need in order to appreciate the poem as a whole.

We took it seriously, but it's true that we are not poets.

Still, because the poems are attached to celebrity, the chat-room reviews have been kind. There is even one woman, Clvlnd_Grl45, who insists that Sarah Pratt-Tipkins is one of her biggest influences. She quotes, here and there, from her favorite pieces. She is sure to tell us that she might not have the poems exactly right.

I know that, sooner or later — if you are still watching — you might try to find her work. I know that you won't find anything. Most of the people watching won't bother checking, and for now there is plenty of proof. We have included citations from various Kansas towns thanking her for charity work, for benefits, for appearances at high schools. In addition to the poems, there are short essays. You can see the obituary, a few poems written by her contemporaries — whom you are more familiar with — in honor of her passing.

And of course there is the house.

When the sun goes back down the interior lighting draws attention to our best work, the slightly darker living room ceiling that makes the space open and intimate at the same time, a quality that a few voices in the chat-room have ascribed to her poems.

If our history does not hold up to scrutiny, it also doesn't wither from it. Proving someone didn't exist is no easy task, especially when, for these thirty-six hours, there is no denying that Sarah Pratt-Tipkins was a very real, exemplary human being.

Looking at the house, reading her work and the small, public reaction to it, I find myself wishing I had been able to meet Sarah, especially when my parents died, or my career ended.

But Sarah Pratt-Tipkins was not alive.

And that's a shame, even if her early work was self-indulgent, even if she never wrote a better book than *Sound*, even if her political conversion was a last ditch effort to assuage guilt from her wasteful Hollywood years.

What I am experiencing, weighing the balance of her unlived life, is a grief undiluted by the baggage of an actual relationship, undiluted by the guilt of having failed her in one way or another. Without the haunting comfort of remembering her face, or how she drank her tea with both hands, I am free to mourn.

Tito is not reverent.

He finds it especially funny when Clvlnd_Grl45, who has been with us for fourteen hours, provides the final stanzas to several of the poems we have excerpted.

But she is not the only one to share in creating the Pratt-Tipkins legacy. Several others are adding gossip, telling us things they think they remember hearing. By the end of our broadcast, Sarah Pratt-Tipkins left behind two ex-husbands and a daughter who may or may not still live in Germany.

With two hours left, we discover that she also left an about-to-be-published manuscript of prose poems that — according to the buzz Manpoet23 heard — take her work in yet another unanticipated direction.

I have Theresa's toothbrush.

By now she has been in California for some time. I am not sure if they will live there, or if they are visiting. On their way somewhere else, up the coast to Portland, perhaps.

Either way, she has seen the ocean now.

A full month after the Pratt-Tipkins broadcast, we are in Ames, Iowa, repainting a house that had been broken into student apartments. We had to buy the whole thing, and wait two weeks for tenants to move out. Nonetheless, it was worth the wait to get the tiny one-bedroom apartment where Tony Newcome wrote *Twice Shy*, his only novel, before he died in 1986 at the age of 24.

We are painting the house into further disrepair, adding a sadness that must have influenced the tone of his lone, great work. The street is busy, a lot of dogs, but no one says hello, and I am able to distract myself with the work.

Wellbutrin is in charge of making paint peel, of half stripping the walls.

He thinks that Newcome died of a heroin overdose. We all agree that Newcome was a user, in his late teens, but Tito and I don't want it to have killed him.

"No one listens to junkies," Tito says.

"We did Burroughs," Wellbutrin says.

"But he didn't die of it," Tito says. "A junkie who dies of something else is a former junkie."

"How about a bee sting?" I ask. "To put so much into your blood and be killed by a bee."

"I still think heroin," Wellbutrin says, pulling on a strip of paint with his fingers. "I don't think people change all that much."

He is looking at Tito when he says it, but Tito doesn't notice.

"The world," Tito says, "doesn't need another story about a black man who destroyed himself."

Wellbutrin and I don't say anything. I was working on the assumption that he was white. We are due for a person of color. I don't know how I feel about forging a racial identity, but there is no question, thinking about it, that Tony Newcome was black.

The broadcast is going as well as can be expected.

There is not as much to talk about, with only the single novel.

Still, there have been almost two hundred people with us the whole time.

As I had hoped, people seem in awe of the ironic bee sting.

There is less focus on the book, though several people claim to have read it. The excerpts we have included are short passages, loaded with imagery, impossible to make sense of as a story. Anyone who summarizes the plot of the novel is intentionally vague.

In terms of race, we are getting a lot of help from strangers. There are a few students and one professor heavily involved in African American Studies who — while they aren't familiar with Newcome — have been great at providing context, and making sense of seemingly contradictory or incongruous biographical elements.

It is about seven in the morning, while the chat room is discussing contemporary implications of race, when I realize that I am less interested in celebrity than I thought. What I am getting from this house has nothing to do with the fake book, the fake notoriety, the fake accomplishments.

Since our dead have never been alive, they are under no obligations to have done anything deserving of fame. History's exacting and discriminating standards for celebrity — the piles and piles of dead white men — can be disregarded completely.

If you are still watching, we can show you anyone.

I am suddenly less interested in changing history than I am in creating a normal life, the small, human details, getting you to imagine the way that Tony Newcome spent his evenings in this place, sober for several years. He often ate radishes with salt and butter. He always wanted a tattoo but could never decide what it should look like.

At about noon of the second day, Livesmart4ever complains that he has been unable to find any of Sarah Pratt-Tipkins's books.

Tito laughs.

Wellbutrin and I turn to each other.

Eventually, Clvlnd_Grl45 suggests a couple of places he should be able to find all of them.

Though Tito has started using the word *hoax* and insulting people in the chat room, Wellbutrin and I are not trying to trick anyone.

We are more than willing for you to find out the truth.

But we want it to be afterwards, after our day-and-a-half wake, so you can mourn the loss. During the actual broadcast, doubt is not an option. After the Newcome broadcast, a few weeks ago, Wellbutrin and I developed a form letter explaining our good intentions, asking for discretion and consideration.

Broadcasting from the house of Tiny Prescott, the poet who died of lung cancer a few years ago, the letter works about half of the time. When it doesn't, Tito has to resort to kicking people out.

Despite our efforts, we are back down to a hundred people.

I am still no more trusting of real history than I am of ours, but it is true that — unlike whoever has constructed more accepted versions of the past — we simply don't have the resources to plant an entire fossil record.

Even with the interlude at the Newcome house Tito has continued to change. What started as efficiency has turned into a radical leanness. He is impatient and pragmatic; he remembers everything. At least five times a day he has good reason to be mad at both Wellbutrin and me.

He has started smoking, and spends most of his time outside, where Wellbutrin and I are hesitant to follow. Even now, as we are broadcasting the tidy split-level, his gaze is out the window, to the streets of Iowa City, where the people are.

We are still at the Prescott house when I suggest we should start doing ordinary people. Though I have more complicated reasons, my argument to them is relatively simple: all of the fact checking distracts our audience from what is important.

"I don't care how many people watch," I say.

"A revolution needs an audience," Tito says.

"I don't care about size," I say, "as long as the audience is attentive, willing to get to know whoever we send them." Wellbutrin nods as I speak, and I can tell I have already won. It is not much of an argument, none of the theoretical positionings of our past.

An hour later, Tito starts teaching Wellbutrin and me how to use the box.

"I'm gonna go," he says. "This isn't what I'm here for. I can get more justice for the dollar somewhere else."

"Like a soup kitchen?" I ask.

He ignores my tone.

"This isn't what any of us signed on for. We're just writers now."

He is leaving us the van and the equipment.

He will not go until he is sure we understand the tech.

When he is finally ready, his good-bye is warmer than anything he has said in some time. I hold him for a while, before leaving him and Wellbutrin to figure out exactly what they are giving up.

"He got his cab," Wellbutrin says, some time later.

Though there is probably more to say, we begin inventing Tammy Joergenson, a special ed. teacher from Apple Valley, Minnesota who died in a car accident on a Thursday, last February. Wellbutrin suggests that her surviving husband might be willing to join us online, to answer any questions, doing his part to help the memory of his wife live on.

Epilogues

This is our last house.

It is not huge, though it seems smaller than it is. It has gabled windows, rooms that are anything but square, and ceilings that slope in unexpected ways. All of the second floor-rooms exit into a small common landing — only eighteen inches wide — that runs next to an open stairwell. The doors leading to the bathroom and second bedroom open at each other; they will not open at the same time.

I am in the bath, an old, footed tub, because we do not have a shower. When Wellbutrin went downstairs, a half-hour ago, his door caught on the handle of mine. I am not sure what he's doing, but he can't hear me.

I am stuck here, naked.

I could dry off and get dressed.

Where I am seems more comfortable.

After Iowa, where Tito left us, we did several houses in Minneapolis. Finally, we decided to come here, to Grand Forks, North Dakota, a place neither of us had ever been. Unlike any of our earlier broadcasts, we are trying to incorporate the surrounding city. We want to be clear that our subjects, two of them this time, were locals.

This is difficult to feign, because we aren't leaving the house.

If we are feeling brave, we can glean some information from whoever delivers us our food, but mostly we have to do research online, conducting surveys and doing interviews. We can see the Red River from one of our windows and we know that it is one of the few rivers in the Northern Hemisphere that flows north. We read it on the city's homepage.

The bathwater is getting cold, so I lift the drain open and run the hot.

I know Wellbutrin will not be long, because we go online at noon. Unlike the other, onetime broadcasts, we do this house in twelve-hour installments. We prepare our food and sleep in the house before we start, taking all of our belongings with us, through a trapdoor in the kitchen, to the dirt-floored basement.

We no longer use a chat-room. I am still hoping we have some kind of audience, but as we started getting more complicated, forging relatives among other things, it became taxing to pay attention to how anyone was responding.

Instead, we continue to post extant journal entries, informative articles, and brief essays in which we postulate what Theresa Muncee and Glen Hughes might have done if they were still alive.

For the first time, we have included pictures.

They are our own, digitally altered.

The Theresa Muncee who died in this house — industrial sabotage when she was ten — has blond hair and smaller eyes than I do.

The Glen Hughes who took his own life at twenty-one looks almost nothing like Wellbutrin. I have asked him if that was his

real name. I have asked him how old he was when he changed it.
I have asked him what happened, what was so terrible.

He says Glen Hughes has nothing to do with him.

He's lying.

All of Theresa Muncie's memories are mine, until age six, when
she didn't hear the advertisement for auditions. From there —
especially in the speculations about how she might have aged —
our lives fork in separate directions.

I hear Wellbutrin in the hallway.

He unbars my door, but doesn't open it.

"I'll be quick," I say.

"You've got time," he says.

When we get to the basement, we will start with today's speculation, how he might have gone fishing with a coworker from the
English department, how she might have played a round of Frisbee
golf before flirting with the man at the used bookstore.

By the time you see it, the tub will be empty and dry.

For the moment, I linger in the water, warmer now.

❧ *About Cover Stories* ❧

In music, a cover is a new version of an old song.

It can be a noun or a verb.

I love covers. I love artists who love covers. I love The Cure covering The Doors. I love Sissy Bar covering Snoop Dogg. I love Pearl Jam covering The Who. I love bands that sound nothing like the bands they are covering. I love bands and artists who take risks, challenging the original song to mean something else and, in fact, become something else. I love Phish covering the entire White Album. I love obscure bluegrass artists covering R&B standards.

The covers I love the most seem to have been written by the cover artist.

When Radiohead does Carly Simon's "Nobody does it Better," the song becomes a Radiohead song, complete with a fuzzy, layered Jonny Greenwood solo that sounds exactly like a fuzzy, layered Jonny Greenwood solo.

And I love it.

In more theoretical language, I have long admired the cover's ability to make meaning in simultaneous ways by conjoining the roles of listener and artist. Implicit in a cover's existence is the decision for the covering artist to cover the song. This reason is often about admiration but not always. This reason is often political but not always.

For me, the cover merges the experiences of creating and enjoying art in a way that few artistic or cultural artifacts do. In fictional terms, several postmodern genres including critifiction have attempted to do similar sorts or things, but they almost always take the form and diction of literary criticism. What I envy about the cover is its ability to make complicated arguments of response in the language of the original art. When Sissy Bar turns the Snoop Doggy Dogg line "got bitches in the living room" into a pretty, harmonious duet sung by two women, the challenge to the original's ethos is striking.

Perhaps as importantly, it's also catchy.

It's criticism that sings.

When I began to study writing academically, I encountered, many times, the theory that there are no new stories; all stories, the theory goes, are one story.

I decided to explore, challenge, reinforce, and defy this idea by hijacking the cover and applying it to fiction. Some would argue that the cover is impossible in fiction because of the lack of the performative element that makes it possible for one song to be recorded in many ways. To that end, I would argue that there is always a difference between a story and how it appears on the page. *Ulysses* would be a very different novel had Hemingway gotten to the story first. Further, *Ulysses* would be a very different novel had Joyce written it ten years later.

Along similar lines, many would argue that the cover already exists in literature. Several examples, including *Ulysses*, come to mind. This is very possible true. However, the bulk of retellings in fiction are obsessed with "standing alone" or supplanting the original in some way, correcting oversights or freeing the story from historical contexts that present difficulties to the contemporary reader. The stories in this collection, while they are meant to be stories, are fairly transparent about the debts they owe to pre-existing stories.

Beyond that, especially given my interest in exploring notions of originality, I would argue that I do not need to be "inventing" the literary cover. I simply wanted to explore it and see what it could do. The stories in this collection vary a great deal in how they cover the original — some change quite a bit of the story, some change only style and voice — but all of them are covers that engage with several of the most important stories and authors in the Western canon.

In the words of Marvin Gaye — words that have been sung or played again by Maceo Parker, The Power Station, Jay Perez, Sistah Sistah, Jack Black, and the World Saxophone Quartet — let's get it on.